BONE JACK

SARA CROWE

BONE JACK

PHILOMEL BOOKS

Philomel Books
An imprint of Penguin Random House LLC
375 Hudson Street
New York, NY 10014

Copyright © 2014, 2017 by Sara Crowe.
First American edition published in 2017 by Philomel Books. Published in
Great Britain by Andersen Press Limited in 2014. Penguin supports copyright.
Copyright fuels creativity, encourages diverse voices, promotes free speech, and
creates a vibrant culture. Thank you for buying an authorized edition of this
book and for complying with copyright laws by not reproducing, scanning, or
distributing any part of it in any form without permission. You are supporting
writers and allowing Penguin to continue to publish books for every reader.

Philomel Books is a registered trademark of Penguin Random House LLC.

Library of Congress Cataloging-in-Publication Data
Names: Crowe, Sara, 1966– author. | Title: Bone Jack / Sara Crowe.
Description: New York, NY : Philomel Books, [2017] | Summary: Ash Tyler
hopes to make his psychologically scarred father proud by training for his town's
Stag Chase, but when he meets the mysterious Bone Jack, dark energies take
root and the world as he knows it is upended. | Identifiers: LCCN 2016025335 |
ISBN 9780399176517 (hardback) | Subjects: | CYAC: Supernatural—Fiction.
| Fathers and sons—Fiction. | BISAC: JUVENILE FICTION / Legends,
Myths, Fables / General. | JUVENILE FICTION / Social Issues / Death &
Dying. | JUVENILE FICTION / Nature & the Natural World / General (see also
headings under Animals). | Classification: LCC PZ7.1.C76 Bo 2017 | DDC
[Fic]—dc23 | LC record available at https://lccn.loc.gov/2016025335

Printed in the United States of America.
9780399176517
10 9 8 7 6 5 4 3 2 1

Edited by Liza Kaplan
Design by Kristin Logsdon
Text set in Parma MT Pro

For my mother and father,
who filled my childhood with stories,
and for Elaine and Joanna,
who encouraged me to write my own.
With love.

IT IS SAID THAT IN ancient times humankind and Nature were as one. Human could take the form of beast and beast could take the form of human. There were spirits in all things, in rock and tree, bird and beast, sun and moon and stars and land. The seasons turned. Some years were years of plenty. Others brought drought or storms or harsh winters that lingered late into spring. In those years, men raced to prove their worth, lest Nature prove her power. But when humankind turns its back on Nature, turns its back on itself, no human nor beast nor the land itself is safe. When humankind turns its back on life, Nature lays its curse. And the old ways return.

STAG'S LEAP. IT FELT LIKE the edge of the world, nothing beyond it but a fall of rock, depth and fierce winds.

Ash Tyler looked down.

Today the wind was hot, as dry and rough as sandpaper against his skin. It tore back his hair, made his eyes stream. He leaned into it, testing its strength against his own.

There was still a foot or so between him and the edge. He inched forward again. The wind slapped his T-shirt around like a sail.

He'd done this before at least a dozen times. Always his best friend Mark's idea. All the crazy things they'd ever done had been Mark's ideas.

Except this time.

Here Ash was again. Alone, with nothing but air between him and a two-hundred-foot fall onto splintered rock.

He stretched out his arms like wings, the way Mark always used to. He forced himself to look down. The salty taste of sweat on his lips. The wind singing in his ears.

The ground seemed to hurtle up toward him and spin away again.

Ash braced himself against the wind. For a few moments

he felt weightless, free, as if he could soar out over the land, ride the air like a hawk. Fly up, pin himself to the sky, watch the blue earth spin beneath him.

He was giddy with fear and joy.

He knew that the wind had only to draw its breath to snatch him away, send him flailing down onto the rocks far below.

He tipped his weight forward until only the balls of his feet tethered him to the ground.

Then the wind dropped.

Ash wobbled. Not much but enough to make fear drill through him. If he fell he'd die, bones shattering, skin ripping against granite, blood on stone.

He tensed. Every sinew wire-taut, every muscle straining.

He hung there for what seemed forever. Then the wind gusted hard again, pushed him upright. He took a step back and then another, sagged down onto the good solid ground.

That had been the closest one yet.

Never again, he told himself. At thirteen, he was too old for these stupid games.

Still trembling from the rush.

Never again.

He rolled onto his back on the parched mountain grass and closed his eyes. The sun was hot on his face. The wind sighed over the mountainside and birds chattered in the thorn trees. Crickets whirred somewhere close by.

Beyond these tiny sounds stretched a vaster silence. Once it would have been broken by the rough cries of sheep, but there weren't any sheep in the mountains anymore. First sickness had weakened them. Then came government men in biohazard suits, the whole area under quarantine, gunshots and terrified bleats shattering the quiet air. Now the sheep were all gone. All dead.

Sometimes Ash imagined he could still smell the stink of blood and burning flesh from the slaughter, the choking disinfectants with which they'd drenched whole farmyards.

The wind dropped again. The air was warm and thick. It clung to his skin like sweat. He sat up, yawned, stretched the tension out of his muscles.

He had a three-mile run home. It was time to get going.

Ash set off at a steady pace down the path. Soon the rhythms of his body took over. He let his thoughts drift apart and fall away until there was only the beat of his feet, the shunt of his lungs and the hard white sky over raw slopes.

The path ran along a crease in the mountain to a wide flattish shoulder halfway down. Brambles, a collapsed dry-stone wall and beyond that a cluster of buildings, the farm where Mark had lived with his family until the bank repossessed it last year.

It had been empty ever since. No one wanted a wind-blasted, run-down hill farm in the aftermath of a foot-and-mouth outbreak.

Ash concentrated on the path. Tried not to look at the farm, not to think about it, not to remember the things he'd seen there. The memories came anyway, dark and airless. Tom Cullen, Mark's dad, up to his neck in debt, silently watching the carcasses of his slaughtered sheep smolder in huge pits. His world falling apart.

"We should have seen it coming," Ash's mom had said

afterward. Eyes full of tears and anger. "We should have done something."

But no one had done anything for Tom Cullen. He'd been too proud to ask for help. That was how it was in the mountains, how it had always been. If things went wrong, you toughed it out and if you told people you were all right, that you didn't need help, they took you at your word and left you to it. Only Tom Cullen's toughness had just been an act and no one had seen through it to realize how desperate he'd become. Not even Mom had seen through it, even though she'd known him for years.

A battered FOR SALE sign hung on the gate. Beyond it was the yard, an expanse of cracked concrete edged with tall weeds and nettles. The farmhouse windows were boarded up. Around it stood several outbuildings, a rusted tractor resting on its wheel rims, a few empty oil drums.

The old barn, its doors hanging on their hinges, its roof sagging.

When they were kids, Ash and Mark had bottle-fed lambs in that barn. Turned the hayloft into a den. Once they'd cornered a marauding fox in there, then, awed by its fierce wildness, stepped back and let it run free into the night.

And in that barn, in the dead of night, Tom Cullen had knotted a rope into a noose, slung it over a beam and—

Ash wouldn't let himself think about that.

Not that.

He ran on and didn't look back. Where the path forked, he took the steeper route, a sharp zigzag downhill between high banks of boulder and thorn.

He came around the shoulder of the mountain and the land opened out before him, greens and grays and purples slashed with fox-red bracken. A wild terrain of deep wide valleys, rough moors, crags.

He liked this route, even though it took him past the Cullen farm. When Dad came home—any day now—they would come running out here together, like they used to. They'd camp at one of the mountain lakes, go canoeing and fishing and rock climbing. They'd worked it all out in e-mails and phone calls.

But lately Dad hadn't been answering his e-mails or his phone and now he was two days late coming home. Mom was worried. She never said so but Ash knew it and so he worried too. The house phone seemed to ring on and off all day but the callers were never Dad.

"Where the hell are you?" Ash said out loud to the mountains and the sky. "Come home, will you?"

He ran faster, remembering another long hot day, sometime last summer, running this route with Dad. For the first time, he'd felt that Dad wasn't holding back so Ash could keep up. He couldn't quite match Dad's pace but he wasn't far behind.

"Only another mile and we're there," Dad said.

"Okay," Ash said. "Pretty soon I'll be leaving you in the dust."

Dad laughed. "I have no doubt. You'll be racing in a year or two, leaving *everyone* in the dust."

And now, a year on, Ash was proving Dad right. There were only two weeks to go until the big race, the annual Stag

Chase through the mountains. It was a local tradition, centuries old, a mix of race and ritual hunt with one boy playing the role of the stag and the others playing the hounds in pursuit. Ash would be the stag boy this year, the lead runner, chased by the other boys. And Dad would be back by then. He'd be there and Ash would win. He had to win, to make Dad proud. Ash was terrible at most sports but he could run like a stag, run like the wild wind. It was the first year he'd been old enough to enter the race and he'd beaten all the other boys in the trials. He would win the Chase, too, and Dad would be waiting at the finish line, brimming with pride.

The whole thing played out like a movie in Ash's mind.

He lengthened his stride, let his body do the thinking, let it make the split-second decisions about footfall and rock and root. Ran through thorn and scrub over slope, stone, ridged mud, slippery patches of wiry grass. The whisper of the breeze, the scrape and scuttle of loose stones underfoot. A kestrel trembling on the high thermals. The burned smell of the sun-scorched land.

A bird shot out of the bracken, then flew straight at Ash's face. A gaping beak the color of steel, ragged black wings, claws ripping at his skin. He flung out his hands, felt feather and bone under his fingers. He staggered, lost his footing and crashed down onto a scratchy mattress of heather.

Then the bird was gone.

Ash rolled onto his back and lay there, breathing hard, heart thumping, staring wide-eyed at a darkening sky.

A FEW SECONDS AGO THE sky had been as pale as the white sun, but now bruised-looking clouds were piling up on each other, a dark avalanche rolling over the land. Still lying on his back, Ash watched it warily. The weather in the mountains could change in the blink of an eye. Last year he'd gotten caught in a brief, ferocious hailstorm that had come out of nowhere on a clear spring day.

Now it looked as if a rainstorm was going to catch him.

He felt a tremor in the mountainside then, a long low vibration like a roll of thunder except that it couldn't be because it didn't stop, just got louder and closer until the bone-dry ground and the air thrummed with it.

Something coming, something powerful and fast. Not only one thing but many, feet pounding the hard earth—animals or people, Ash couldn't tell which.

Whatever they were, they were coming uphill toward him.

Ash scrambled to his feet, looked around.

Nothing.

But there was still something coming, the pounding getting louder, closer. He backed away from the path into dense scrub that tore at his bare legs. He couldn't run through that, couldn't get any farther away from the path.

He looked for somewhere to hide, but now a stone skittered at the bend below. Behind it came a running boy. He was about Ash's age—thirteen, maybe fourteen—and he was tall and lean like Ash too, wearing rough brown leggings and thin leather boots like some ancient-days character from a movie or a computer game. In the heat haze he seemed almost spectral. His hair was sculpted into spikes stiffened with pale mud or clay. More clay caked his face, made a cracked and peeling mask. Above the waist he was naked except for a crude design daubed on his chest, a bloodred stag's head with branching antlers. He stumbled as he ran, lurched and flailed, staggered onward again. His eyes were wide with terror. His clay face stretched into a silent scream.

The boy was exhausted. Ash could see that right away. Beyond exhausted. Legs heavy. His head bobbing, breathing in quick wheezy gasps.

But he kept running.

Like he was running for his life.

His gaze met Ash's as he passed but he didn't stop, didn't break his stumbling stride.

Still there was the rumble in the mountainside, stronger now. Ash crouched down low, waited with his breath catching in his throat, hoped whatever was coming up the path wouldn't notice him hiding amid the bracken and thorn trees.

The boy was out of sight now.

Time crawled.

Then more boys appeared farther down the mountain. First three or four, then dozens of them streaming into view. As with the first boy, there was something weird about them, as if they were tricks of the light. They wore leggings, masks, thin leather boots strapped at the ankle. But their masks weren't clay. Theirs were ragged creations of painted, stiffened sackcloth, masks with eyeholes slashed into them and gaping mouths. Their pace was steady and relentless. They looked as if they could run all day. Soon they'd catch up with the fleeing boy and his race would be over.

Ash knew what they were. Their costumes were wrong, but these were hound boys and this was a Stag Chase. Except it couldn't be. The Stag Chase was only held once a year and it wasn't for another two weeks. The stag boy fleeing the hounds was supposed to be Ash. Not this clay-daubed stranger.

The runners passed Ash as if he wasn't there: ten, twenty, thirty and more of them.

A pack of hounds, running their prey to the ground.

The stag boy didn't stand a chance. They'd catch up with him on the ridge, perhaps even sooner.

Ash tensed, about to jump up and help him. Then he stopped. The strangeness of the hounds unnerved him and there were too many of them anyway. Already they were almost out of sight, only the stragglers still visible as the path jackknifed its way up the mountain.

Ash stood still, heart hammering, watching the last boy slip beyond a curve in the path.

Then a shriek ripped through the silence: part human, part animal.

The stag boy. It had to be. The hounds must have caught up with him by Stag's Leap.

9

The blood drained from Ash's face.

Something terrible was happening. He knew it in his bones, as surely as he knew night from day. No one screamed like that except from raw terror. This wasn't just a race. This was dark, savage, murderous. A hunt, with the stag boy as its prey.

Ash left his hiding place in the undergrowth and crept back to the path, ran a little way along it, then scrambled up onto a swell of higher ground to get a better view. He scanned the upper slopes for the boy and the hounds.

They couldn't have gotten farther than that. There hadn't been enough time.

But there was no sign of them.

Not a sound, not a movement.

They were gone.

The storm clouds had vanished too, sucked back over the horizon. Instead the glaring white-metal sky stretched from horizon to horizon again, so bright it hurt Ash's eyes.

A tiny movement farther up the mountainside caught his attention. He shielded his eyes and squinted into the sunlight.

There was a girl standing on a boulder, watching him. Her hair was dark and wild. She wore a dress the dusty red of roadside poppies. He recognized her right away: Callie Cullen, Mark's younger sister.

Relief flooded through Ash at the sight of someone familiar. Suddenly everything seemed ordinary again. The impossible Stag Chase gone, the world settling back to its sensible self.

It struck him that Callie must have seen the running boys too, must have seen where they went.

"Callie!" he hollered. "Hey! Did you see those runners? Where did they go?"

If she heard him, she didn't answer. She stood there, watching him, motionless except for the breeze tugging at her dress and hair.

Ash gazed back at her for a long moment, then he gave up. Everything that had happened this morning was too weird. All he wanted now was to be back at home, in his own room, where things made sense and he could shut the door, lose himself in a computer game, keep the world at arm's length. Soon Dad would be home, maybe even today, and everything would be all right.

Nothing else mattered.

Ash set off at an unsteady trot, still shaky with adrenaline. His legs sloshed around as if they were full of water.

Heat shimmered on the mountainside, split the air, played tricks on his eyes. Faraway things seemed close; close things seemed farther than they really were. And shadows raced alongside him, like the shadows of scudding clouds. Except there weren't any clouds, not anymore, just the white-hot sky stretching from horizon to horizon.

The shadows spooked Ash. He didn't look back. Instead he ran harder, faster, and he didn't stop until he reached home.

3

MOM WAS WORKING IN THE garden when Ash got back. Wearing her frayed straw hat, harvesting corn from plants as tall, slender and disheveled-looking as she was. He waved at her through the kitchen window, watched her for a while.

Life was getting back to normal, bit by bit. Just Dad missing.

Ash poured two glasses of orange juice and took them outside.

Mom had been busy. A heaped basket stood at her feet.

"Impressive crop, Mom," said Ash.

"It's about the only one that's done well in this drought. So we'll be having corn with every meal for the next month." She pushed a loose strand of her pale hair back under her hat and smiled at him. "Including breakfast."

"Bacon, eggs and corn? Gross. What's wrong with the corn that comes in cans?"

She laughed and tidied his wind-wild hair, the way she used to when he was small. He groaned in protest but didn't pull away.

She let him go. She sipped her juice, set the glass down

next to the basket and twisted off another ear of corn. "Did you have a good run?"

Ash hesitated. He wanted to tell her about the bird flying into his face, about the stag boy being hunted down, how the running boys seemed to vanish into thin air, the freaky storm clouds, the shadows that had chased him. But when the words formed in his mind, it all sounded creepy and unreal, a crazy dream best kept to himself.

She had enough to worry about anyway, with Dad still not back.

"Yeah, it wasn't bad," he said. "I went up to Stag's Leap. I saw Callie up there."

"Callie?" Mom stopped breaking the corn ears from their stalks and gave him her full attention. "Was Mark with her?"

"No. It was just her."

"What was she doing out there by herself? Did you talk to her?"

"I tried but she wouldn't talk to me."

"Huh," said Mom. "Those poor kids."

Ash's face grew hot. He didn't need the reminder.

"Have you thought about trying to make friends with Mark again?" she asked.

"I've tried lots of times." It wasn't exactly a lie—he had made an effort after Mark's dad hanged himself, at first. But bad things seemed to collect around Mark after his dad died. Dark and violent things that unnerved Ash. So when Mark pushed him away, Ash let himself be pushed, and then time passed and their friendship got awkward. These days they barely saw each other.

He couldn't explain all that to Mom. She wouldn't get it. She'd tell him not to be so superstitious and silly. There'd be disappointment in her eyes, in her voice.

Ash couldn't stand that.

He cleared his throat and changed the subject. "Has Dad called yet?"

Stupid question. If he had called, she'd have told him by now.

"Not yet," said Mom. "I'm sure he'll be home soon, though."

Her voice suddenly sounded too cheerful.

Ash drained his glass of juice. "Right. Think I'll go take a shower."

He stood in the shower for a long time, letting the hot water sluice away the sweat and dust from his run. Then he toweled himself dry, went up to his bedroom in the attic and put on fresh clothes.

Through the open bedroom window, he heard the garden gate shriek on its hinges.

It was probably just the mailman, he told himself. But his heart leaped anyway and he rushed to the window.

It wasn't the mailman.

It was Dad.

DAD WAS STANDING IN THE driveway, near the gate. He looked the way Ash remembered: tall, broad-shouldered, tough as teak. He was dressed in civilian clothes and his dark hair was starting to grow out of the regulation army cut, but he still looked like a soldier through and through.

Captain Robert Tyler, home from war.

Then Dad walked out onto the lawn and it all started to fall apart. He looked loose somehow, as if his bones weren't properly connected. Dragging his feet, swaying, stumbling.

Like a puppet with its strings cut.

Ash watched from above and a tiny knife of anxiety twisted inside him.

In the middle of the lawn, Dad stopped. He stared at the house as if it was somewhere he remembered from a dream. Then he looked straight up at the open window where Ash stood.

Ash stuck out his head. "Dad! Hey!"

Dad went on staring, as if Ash was a stranger to him. No smile, no wave, not even a flicker of recognition.

Ash flinched as if he'd been slapped across the face.

Dad took another step, lurched sideways, almost fell.

Drunk, thought Ash. Or maybe something else was wrong, something worse.

Anxiety cut through him again.

He ran down the stairs but stopped short just inside the front door.

Mom had come around the side of the house. She was still wearing her old straw hat. She stopped for a long moment, watching Dad. He hadn't noticed her. He was still staring up at the house as if he'd never seen it before. She called out to him, her voice soft and low and so full of love that Ash suddenly felt afraid for her. For all of them.

Dad looked across at her. He smiled weirdly, then a sob broke from him and he buckled, seemed about to crumple to his knees on the grass. Then Mom was running toward him and she caught him in her arms, held him close, held him up.

Ash turned away, embarrassed. Suddenly they didn't seem like his parents anymore. Instead they were like two strangers caught in the middle of something huge and terrible that he didn't understand, didn't want to see.

He went back to his room and sat down on his bed, lay back, stared at the ceiling.

A door slammed downstairs. He closed his eyes. A bloodred glare spread behind his eyelids, with circling specks of black that opened dark wings and flapped away like carrion crows over a battlefield.

He curled up into a ball, rocked himself for a while, opened his eyes again.

"Ash!" his mother called.

However much he wanted to, he couldn't stay up here forever. Sunshine outside, Dad home at last. The Stag Chase only two weeks away. Everything waiting for him. So Ash got up and went downstairs.

They were sitting at the kitchen table, mugs of tea in front of them. Typical, Ash thought. Their lives were falling apart and Mom, trying to hold it all together, had made a pot of tea.

Dad looked exhausted. Bruises under his eyes, his skin too thin and too tight, grayish under his desert tan. He glanced at Ash and then away again.

He looked ill too. Injured, maybe, Ash thought. But the army would have told them if Dad had been injured, so it couldn't be that. Still, it seemed more than drunkenness. He'd seen Dad drunk before. Not often, but enough to know that this was different in some dark, deeper way that Ash didn't understand.

"Your dad's home," said Mom. As if Dad wasn't sitting right next to her.

"I know," said Ash. He tried to smile, to make light of it. "I can see him."

He pulled out a chair. The chair legs screeched across the linoleum and Dad winced.

"How are you doing, Dad?" Ash asked.

Silence except for the tick of the wall clock.

"I've been out in the mountains, running a lot," Ash continued. "Along all the old routes you showed me." Wildly, he imagined that if he just talked to Dad, acted as if everything

17

was normal, then somehow it would really become that way—Dad would be his old self again and everything would be wonderful now that he was home.

That was how it was supposed to be when your dad came back after months away at war. Family time. Hugs and laughter and love. A reunion and a celebration.

But Ash didn't know what else to say.

Silence filled the room. For a while they sat there, unspeaking and awkward until Dad's eyes half closed and he slumped a bit in his chair, almost slid off it onto the floor, grabbed the edge of the table to save himself. Tea slopped out of the mugs.

"He's drunk," said Ash, before he could stop the words. "He stinks of beer."

"That's enough, Ash," said Mom sharply. "You're not helping."

He looked at her, looked at Dad, and suddenly found himself blinking away tears.

"I'm tired," said Dad, to no one in particular. His words slurring together. "If you don't mind, I need to sleep now."

He stood up. So did Mom. "Here, let's get you upstairs," she said.

"No!" Dad's voice cracking out like a whip. Mom looking on in shock. "Sorry," he said. "I'm sorry. I just . . . need some time to myself. Some sleep. I'll be better tomorrow."

Then he lurched upstairs to the spare room with his backpack as if he were a guest.

And Ash knew he wouldn't be better tomorrow.

MORNING.

The distant mountains looked like a watercolor dissolving in rain, colors running together. But it was the heat haze that made the air flicker and blur, not the rain. There hadn't been any rain for almost two months. The grass was brittle and burned golden brown and the streams had shrunk to sluggish trickles that were more mud than water. Everything was tired, wilting, dusty, and Ash felt the same way, felt a hundred years old, as if all his strength and energy had been leached out.

He had a shopping list and money in his pocket. He knew the shopping was just Mom's excuse to get him out of the house but he didn't care. Even though Dad had only been home for one night, it was a relief to get out for a while. A relief not to be at home with Dad in such rough shape, not to be saying stupid things like he had yesterday. Ash was better off away from all of it.

He headed past the park and playground, toward the row of little shops on the other side of the main street.

Then he saw her, sitting on one of the swings. Callie, barefoot and still wearing the dusty red dress he'd seen her in yesterday. Her serious gray eyes watched Ash. He got the feeling she'd been waiting for him. But she couldn't have been. She couldn't have known that Mom would send him out to the shops.

Ash walked over and sat on the swing next to hers. He breathed in the smells of hot tarmac, rubber, old bubblegum. Playground smells.

"I saw you yesterday," he said. "Out in the mountains, up by Stag's Leap."

She stared at him. "So what?"

The edge of dislike in Callie's voice shocked him. They'd never been friends exactly, but she'd always been there, at the edge of his life, a quiet, serious girl with a slow, shy smile.

Ash had always thought she liked him just fine, as much as he'd thought about her at all. Now she sounded like she almost hated him.

He bit his lip, looked away. After a while he said, "Did you see anyone else out there?"

"Like who?"

"Like runners," he said. "Lots of them. Hound boys."

"No, I didn't see anyone."

"They ran up the path to the top of the ridge. They must have run right past you."

"I thought the Stag Chase wasn't for another two weeks?"

"It's not."

"So then they couldn't have been hound boys. Anyway, I didn't see them. I didn't see anyone up there except you."

"You're lying," he said. He was sure of it. There was no way Callie could have missed the runners. Ash expected her to get angry and deny it but she didn't. She gave him a look that said she didn't really care what he thought.

Somehow that was worse. It meant that maybe she was telling the truth and he was the only one who had seen the runners. And if he was the only one who'd seen them, then maybe he'd imagined them. Maybe they'd never been there at all.

Maybe he'd been seeing things—mirages—like people saw in deserts. Tricks of the light.

Ash tilted his weight a little. The swing moved. His feet scraped across the ground.

"I heard you and Mark moved in with your grandpa," he said.

A guarded look. "Yeah, we stay there sometimes."

"Only sometimes? Where do you stay the rest of the time?"

She shrugged, gazed off into the distance. "Here and there."

She wasn't making this easy, but still he kept trying. "How's Mark doing?"

"What do you care?"

That was it, Ash knew. The reason for the anger that kept coming back into her voice. She thought he'd betrayed Mark, abandoned him when Mark needed him the most. As far as Callie was concerned, that made Ash the enemy.

He didn't blame her for feeling that way.

"I couldn't . . ." he said, stumbling over the words. "Look, Callie. Everything changed after your dad died. Mark changed. He was like a stranger. I didn't know what to do. I didn't know what to say to him."

"What did you expect?" said Callie. "We lost our mom and then Dad killed himself and we lost the farm. We lost everything. Mark got strange and crazy." She looked straight at Ash. "But he was still Mark."

"I'm sorry."

"Saying you're sorry doesn't help. It's just a word you say to make yourself feel better."

"I don't feel better."

"Well, good. You don't deserve to."

Ash didn't know how to respond so he said nothing.

Callie continued. "You were supposed to be his best friend. When you got bullied at school, Mark always stuck up for you. But when he needed you, you gave up on him."

"I'm sorry," he said again.

Callie shook her head and looked away. "He wants to see you," she said. "That's why I'm here. I was going to stop by your house later."

"What does he want?"

"I don't know. He's the one who wants to see you, not me."

"Okay. Well, when?"

"Tomorrow night. It has to be tomorrow night."

"I don't think I can come tomorrow." Not when Dad has only been home a day, he thought. But he couldn't tell Callie that, couldn't tell her that his dad had returned safely from war when her own dad was dead. And why did it have to be tomorrow? Ash wondered.

"You haven't changed," she said. "You're still useless."

"Maybe next week. It's just . . . I can't get to your grandpa's house tomorrow. I'm sorry. My mom's busy so I won't have a ride." Immediately he reddened at the excuse. It was only a few miles to Coldbrook, where Mark and Callie's grandpa lived. Callie knew as well as Ash did that it would take him less than half an hour on his bike.

"He's not staying at Grandpa's," she said. "He's hardly ever there."

"Oh. Why does it have to be tomorrow, anyway?"

"Because that's when he wants to see you," she said. "Because next week might be too late."

"Too late for what?"

"All I know is it has to be tomorrow night," she said again, looking away. "That's what Mark said."

"I can't. There's stuff going on at home. Mom needs me there."

"I know your dad's back," she said. "You don't have to lie."

He stared at her, shocked. "How do you know he's back?"

"You know what it's like around here," she said. "Everyone knows everyone else's business."

"Seriously, who told you?"

"Relax. No one told me. I saw the taxi drop him off at the top of your street yesterday. Then he walked toward your house. He looked . . . bad."

"Drunk," said Ash. "He was drunk."

"He probably had his reasons."

"Yeah, well, whatever. He's still a mess."

Callie shot Ash a strange look and this time he glowered back at her. He'd had enough. He made a move to leave but she stopped him.

"You're an idiot, Ash."

"What?"

"Your dad just got back from a war." She spoke slowly, as if she was explaining something very simple to someone very stupid. "Think about what he must have seen. He must have been shot at, seen bombs going off. He probably saw people getting killed. His own men, and enemy fighters, and ordinary people who got in the way. Old people. Women. Kids."

The muscles in Ash's jaw were so tense they ached.

"Look up post-traumatic stress disorder on the Internet when you get home," said Callie. "Look up survivor guilt."

"Oh yeah? And what makes you the expert?"

"We studied it in school last year. World War I. A lot of soldiers in the trenches got PTSD. You must have studied it too, the year before me."

"Whatever," Ash said, tight-lipped.

"I'll wait for you at the Monks Bridge tomorrow night at nine," she said. "If you come, I'll take you to Mark. If you don't, he'll never ask you again."

Ash sighed. "I'll try," he said.

He remembered the shopping list in his pocket and stood to leave. The swing creaked on its chains, knocked against the backs of his legs. He began walking away.

"Those runners," Callie called after him. "The hound boys you said you saw—you should ask Mark about them."

"Why? What would he know about them?"

"He knows everything that goes on in the mountains. Ask him."

• • •

Ash crossed the road to the little grocery shop. There was a poster in the window, a stylized stag's head in bloodred paint against a black background. SHARE IN THE EXCITEMENT OF THORNDITCH'S HISTORIC STAG CHASE, the poster said. A thrill ran through him. For a moment, nothing else mattered—not Dad, not Mark. Just that Ash was the stag boy, that he'd won the trials, beaten all the other boys. All eyes would be on him at the start of the race. His heart quickened at the thought of it. He'd run and he'd win and he'd be a hero for the first time in his life. The boys at school would have no reason to pick on him anymore.

Ash went inside the shop. He wandered along narrow strips of ancient checkered linoleum between high walls of shelving stacked with canned soup, boxes of cereal, toilet paper. The hum of the refrigerator in the back. Reedy voices on the radio that old Mr. Linnet listened to as he sat on his chair behind the wooden counter with its lottery card display and candy bars. It all seemed exactly the same as it had been ever since Ash could remember.

Today it felt like the only still point at the center of a chaotic universe.

He took his time gathering the items on Mom's shopping list: eggs, bread, milk.

"Ready for the Stag Chase?" said Mr. Linnet.

"Yeah, I think so."

"I remember when your dad was the stag boy. Must be twenty years ago now. There was a drought that year too,

25

as I recall. Not half as bad as this one, though. How is your dad, anyway?"

"He's all right. He's home. Got back yesterday."

"He'll be coming to watch you run, then. He must be very proud of you."

Ash faked a smile. "Yeah, I guess so."

As he watched Mr. Linnet ring up his items, the hairs on the back of his neck prickled as if there was something out there, in the hard sunlight outside. Something watching, waiting.

Ash looked up.

Five faces were pressed against the window—faces as blank as masks. Older boys he recognized from school, boys from Coldbrook.

He stared back at them, unnerved.

"Is that everything?" said Mr. Linnet.

Ash tore his gaze from the boys outside. "Huh?"

"Your shopping," said Mr. Linnet. "Have you got everything you wanted?"

"Oh. Yeah, thanks." Ash fumbled in his pockets for the cash from Mom. When he looked up again, the boys were gone. Only a movement across the street, a flap of black as if the breeze had caught the tail of someone's coat as they swung around a corner. Then there was nothing except a crow shaking out its feathers on a wall before winging away into the pale sky.

6

AT LUNCHTIME MOM MADE LASAGNA and loaded a tray for Dad.

"He hasn't eaten so much as a bite since he got back," she said.

"I'll take it up to him if you want," said Ash.

She hesitated.

"It'll be fine, Mom. Let me do it."

Ash knocked before he entered Dad's room. There was no answer but he went in anyway. It was pitch-black in there, the heavy curtains pulled so tight that not even a thread of light showed. The air smelled of sweat and unwashed clothes.

"Dad, I'm going to turn the light on, okay?"

A grunt from across the room.

Ash flipped the switch.

Dad was on the hard twin bed, adrift among all the random bits of furniture and junk stored in the room because they didn't fit anywhere else. He was lying on his side, facing the wall with the sheet pulled up to his ears. His backpack was on the floor nearby, clothes spilling out of it.

Ash put down the tray on a small table by the door and dragged it over to the bed.

"Mom made lunch for you. Lasagna."

Dad turned over in the bed and his eyes opened a crack. "Thanks. Just leave it there."

"You getting up?"

"In a bit."

"You'll feel better if you get up." Ash hovered by the bed. He trawled his mind for something more to say. "You could come out running with me tomorrow. If you want."

Silence. Then Dad mumbled, "Maybe next week."

Next week. Or never. Then Ash remembered. He hadn't told Dad yet that he'd entered the Stag Chase, that he'd won the trials and would be the stag boy in this year's race. It was supposed to be a surprise, his great gift to Dad on his homecoming.

He should tell him now.

But he couldn't. The timing was all wrong. In the state he was in, Dad would barely even register the news. And it had to be big, it had to be special.

Ash drew a deep slow breath, exhaled again. "All right," he said. "Next week, then."

"Sure. Maybe."

"Right." Ash paused. "Do you want me to leave the light on?"

"No. Turn it off, please. I want to sleep."

Ash stood there for a few moments. Swallowed the lump that had formed in his throat. He felt useless, helpless. There was an abyss yawning between him and Dad and all he could think of was the lasagna congealing, the salad wilting, the roll going dry and hard. He told himself it didn't matter. It was only food.

But somehow it did matter.

"Mom made it special for you," he said. "It's what you always want when you get home."

Dad grunted.

"You need to eat, Dad."

"I will eat."

"You won't. You'll leave it and it'll get disgusting."

"I said I'll eat it," said Dad. Pulling the sheet up over his head, mumbling through the cotton. "Later."

Ash started to leave.

"I'll be better tomorrow," said Dad.

"Yeah," said Ash. "Tomorrow." He didn't need to remind his dad he had made the same promise yesterday.

He turned off the light, closed the door behind him and went up to his bedroom.

He sat at his desk, staring at the photographs pinned to the corkboard above it. Him and Dad home from a long hike, tired and dusty and hungry and happy. Dad teaching him how to roll a canoe in a mountain lake. Dad on one of the climbing expeditions he used to go on with his army buddies when he was younger. Up on some mountain, blue sky beyond. Dad was tanned, squinting into the sun, smiling like he didn't have a care in the world.

More than anything, Ash wanted the Dad in the photograph back—strong and capable, always up for adventure.

But that Dad was gone. For now. Or maybe forever.

Ash's gaze traveled over the other pictures on the corkboard. A print of a leaping wolf he'd cut from a magazine; an eerie photograph of a fox on a misty moonlit night; a black-and-white shot of Stag's Leap, raw and mysterious under a stormy sky. A picture of him and Mark, taken at the farm a year and a half ago. They'd gone mountain biking that day, finding the steepest routes and shredding their bikes along the dirt track down the eastern flank of Tolley Carn Peak. They were mud-spattered and grinning, their eyes full of light and laughter. Ash smiled at the memory. He hadn't wanted to go. Mark had dared him, goaded him, then, suddenly gentle, said, "You can do it. You'll be okay. I know you will." And Ash had done it, taut with fear through the whole crazy, hurtling descent but he'd made it and afterward he'd felt exhilarated and free, invincible.

It seemed like a lifetime ago.

Ash looked away. He booted up the laptop and opened the web browser.

He typed *post-traumatic stress disorder* into the search engine. He vaguely remembered learning about it in school but he hadn't paid much attention. Now it seemed important that he know more.

Hundreds of hits came up: medical sites, psychology sites, sites about World Wars I and II, Vietnam, the Falklands, Afghanistan, Iraq. Help groups for veterans. Videos.

He clicked on a video link. Grainy black-and-white film from a century ago, soldiers who'd fought in the trenches and survived. Men who returned home from war shaking and twitching, wide-eyed with terror, as if the war was still raging around them and shrapnel might rip through flesh and bone at any moment.

A soldier hiding his face, trying to get away from the camera, trotting jerkily in frightened circles.

Like a beaten dog.

Ash couldn't watch any more. He slammed the laptop shut, sat staring at the wall, seeing nothing.

Slowly he came back to himself. His eyes focused on a small picture he'd hung up, of the Stag Chase from twenty years ago, the year Dad had been the stag boy. There he was, outside the Huntsman Inn in Thornditch, wearing the ancient antler headdress that the stag boy paraded in if he won his race. He looked uncomfortable, stiffly posed, his expression solemn instead of triumphant.

Dad must have been about fifteen back then. Two years older than Ash was now. He was powerfully built even at that age. He didn't have a distance runner's physique like Ash did. In fact, Ash didn't look like him at all. He had Mom's fair hair and her slender, bony frame. He wasn't strong like Dad, wasn't a fighter. But he had his dad's eyes, blue and intense.

Ash took the photograph down from the corkboard and looked at it more closely. There were hound boys in the background, prowling predatory youths still acting out their roles even after the race was over.

They seemed more hound than boy.

One of them stood apart from the others. His mask was pushed back on top of his head. Tom Cullen, Mark and Callie's dad. He was smiling, his face not yet set into the stern lines that Ash remembered.

Ash pinned the photograph back onto the corkboard.

Too much thinking.

He needed to do something other than sit there with his mind spinning. He got up and scooped up his dirty running gear to dump it in the laundry basket.

Something fell to the floor.

It was a feather, about six inches long. Black, with a metallic purple sheen that shimmered in the light like oil on water. Ash remembered the bird that had flown into him on the mountain path. The brittle touch of its hollow bones, its inky feathers. One of those feathers must have snagged on his clothing.

And now it was here, in his bedroom, a fragment of darkness he'd accidentally brought back with him. He stared at it so long that it started to lose its shape, blurring at the edges, leaking shadow that joined up with other shadows, spreading like a dense black mist across the floor.

He had to get rid of it. But that meant he'd have to go closer to it, touch it, hold it. The thought made his skin crawl. He took a step toward it, felt a dark pull, a sickening depth opening before him. Another step, and another. Ash stopped and bent down. Turned his face away from it, half closed his eyes. Held his breath. His fingertips brushed over the carpet, over the feather. He forced himself to pick it up.

His head swam. He lurched and swayed, slammed his hand against the wall for balance. He closed his eyes tightly until the nausea subsided.

Seconds later the room was itself again. The feather no more than a feather.

But there was no way he could bear to see or touch it any longer. He shoved it into a pocket of his backpack and put the backpack on the landing, outside his bedroom door.

He'd get rid of the feather tomorrow, somewhere far from the house.

THE NEXT NIGHT, ASH FOUND Callie waiting for him at the Monks Bridge, as she'd promised. The red dress was gone, replaced with cargo pants and a fleece that looked three sizes too big for her.

He was nervous to go, but things at home were no better and he wanted to ask Mark about the hound boys he'd seen.

Except there was no sign of Mark.

A ghostly crescent moon sat low above the trees. Bats flitted through the smoky blue dusk, quick blinks of shadow. Below the bridge the little river slid along, as sleek and brown as an otter.

After a moment, Ash said, "Well, I'm here. Where's Mark?"

Callie watched Ash, her eyes as silver as the moonlight. "I'll take you to him. Come on."

"Wait," he said. "There's something I have to do first."

Ash took the feather out of his backpack. In the half-light, it looked like nothing, just an ordinary black feather. No shadows spreading from it, no cold dread chilling Ash's blood. Perhaps his mind had been playing tricks on him after all.

Either way, he was determined to get rid of it.

He leaned over the side of the bridge and dropped it. It was gone in an instant, swept away by the fast water below.

"Okay," he said. "We can go now."

"What was that?" said Callie.

"A feather."

She shot him a sideways look. "A feather?"

"It's not important," he said. He shrugged as if it was no big deal. "So are you taking me to see Mark or what?"

"This way," she said, and set off along the road.

They were half a mile out of the village on a road that bucked and twisted along the mountainside, linking farmhouses. "We'll have to go across the fields part of the way," said Callie.

"Where to?"

"It doesn't have a name."

"Everywhere has a name."

"If it does, I don't know it. It's just a patch of woodland."

"How much farther is it?"

"Not far."

They trudged along, Callie a few paces ahead. She didn't speak, didn't even look at Ash and, in her silence, he again sensed her disapproval of him.

"It must have been hard for you when your dad died," he said. Immediately he cringed inside at his own words. Lately almost everything that came out of his mouth sounded wrong.

"Look," she said, "I don't want to talk about that stuff. I'm taking you to Mark, that's all, because he wants to talk to you. And you used to be his best friend so maybe you can help him, but you probably can't. Anyway, he wants to see you and that's the only reason I'm here."

Her words cut. *Used to be.* "Fine," Ash muttered.

They veered from the road, climbed up and over a stile in thickening gloom. As Ash's eyes adjusted to the darkness, he could make out a faint path around the edge of the field. An untidy hedge to his left. Long grass spiked with thistles to his right.

Beyond the field, woodland stretched like a dark wound around the foot of the mountain.

They paused close to the tree line. A twig snapped close by. A low bough jerked and shook its leaves. Ash stared into the murk, his heart jumping. "What was that?"

"Just the wild," Callie said.

He looked at her. Suddenly she seemed like a wild creature herself, as silent and secret as a fox slipping through the night. The thought made Ash shiver.

Ash smelled smoke from a wood fire and now, as the path took them on through the trees, he saw firelight flicker deep in the clotted shadows.

Callie stopped. "That's Mark's campfire over there," she said. "He's around here somewhere."

"Aren't you coming with me?"

She shook her head. "He wants to talk to you alone."

He watched Callie turn and go, her slight figure becoming a shadow that melted away into the night until at last it swallowed her and Ash was alone.

Except for Mark.

Ash went deeper into the woods, then stopped in his tracks, his breath catching in his throat. A gaunt white face stared down at him, long and bony, its eyes hollow with night.

Beyond it, other faces gleamed in the dark, a dozen or more of them.

Then he realized what they were and started to back away. Skulls, sheep skulls. Some wedged in the forks of branches, others stuck up on sticks driven into the ground or turning slowly at the ends of strings tied around boughs. Three dead crows, feet bound together, swinging from a branch. Feathers blacker than the fire-cut dark, black as the feather Ash had found in his bedroom.

And behind the crows and the skulls monstrous shadows shifted among the trees, a dozen or more of them, eerily silent. Figures in masks, distorted and weird, throwing out their long limbs, leaping, plunging, twisting.

Freaky shadow people dancing like crazed shamans around a fire.

Mark had company.

Ash dropped into a crouch behind a tree and watched them dance. They were quick and agile, soaring up, spinning, tangling, tearing apart, re-forming and sinking to the ground only to leap up again.

Ash's heart thumped so loudly he was sure they could hear it.

It's only people dancing, he told himself. It's only hound boys dressed up in their costumes. Boys, and shadows thrown by the firelight.

But fear ran through him. The dancing boys seemed both more than human and somehow less so at the same time. Half boy and half beast, and as dark as the night.

And Mark was in there with them.

Maybe this was just a game, the usual ritual in the lead-up to the Chase, when the hound boys tormented the stag boy and tried to unnerve him to give the race a dangerous edge.

And Mark was expecting him. Ash couldn't get out of it. He'd look like a coward and an idiot if he ran away or crouched behind a tree all night.

He drew a deep breath to steady his nerves, then stood up and walked out into the clearing.

His arrival seemed to shatter a spell. The shadowy boys spun away into the night. They didn't go far, though, he was sure of that. Ash sensed them still out there, lurking among the trees, beyond the circle of firelight. Watching him.

Now, at last, he saw Mark. He was standing in front of the fire, facing it. He was dressed in loose, torn trousers and nothing else. His hair was matted and spiked with pale clay, his body caked with it.

Ash had seen that look before, on the stag boy running in the mountains.

"Mark," he said, walking toward the fire. "Hey. It's me. Ash. Callie brought me. She said you wanted to talk to me."

Mark turned. His face was a cracked clay mask. There were charcoal smudges around his eyes. Skull-faced, death-faced. His grin flashed bright and fierce in the firelight. "Ash," he said. "You came. I thought you'd chicken out."

"Yeah," said Ash. "I almost did."

Mark nodded. His gaze slid away toward the trees on the other side of the fire.

"What's with the zombie look?" said Ash.

Mark turned to face him again. He raised his arms

straight out in front of him, slackened his jaw, took a few stiff-legged steps toward Ash. "Mwahahaha! I smell fresh meat. Human meat. Mwahahaha!"

Ash laughed. "You're still an idiot," he said. He looked around. "Where did the other boys go?"

Mark dropped his arms back down to his sides.

"Those boys who were leaping around the fire a minute ago," Ash continued. "All dressed up in hound costumes. They ran off when I got here. Who were they? Why did they run off like that?"

Mark shrugged and cocked his head. "You tell me."

"Stop playing games," said Ash. "You got Callie to bring me out here so you could talk to me. So say whatever it is you have to say."

"You think you're so special, don't you?" said Mark. "Because you're the stag boy, but you don't even know what that means, not really. You don't know anything about the Stag Chase. You don't know its history. You're not fit to be the stag boy."

"I know as much as you do," said Ash.

"What do you know? Go on, tell me."

Suddenly Ash's mind was blank. He fumbled for words, facts. "It's ancient," he said. "It's been held every year since . . . since before the Romans. It's a ritual for good hunting and a good harvest and . . ."

His voice trailed off. Mark laughed.

"Tell me, then," said Ash. "If you think you know it all."

Abruptly Mark's eyes hardened and his mocking smile

twisted into a snarl. He took three long, running leaps at Ash, flung out his fist, gave him a hammer blow to the jaw. Ash staggered backward, his legs collapsing under him. His mouth flooded with the thin taste of metal. He gagged and spat blood.

Mark loomed over him. "This isn't a game," he said.

"What the hell?" said Ash. "I don't know what you're talking about."

He was on all fours on the forest floor, the dry mulch of last year's leaf-fall crunching under his weight. His mouth felt thick and raw. His voice sounded as if it was rolling over pebbles.

"You're the stag boy," said Mark. "Do you think it's just about winning a race?"

"Yeah," said Ash. "Just like it was last year and every year before that."

"Mostly it's about winning a race," said Mark. Softer now, and deadly serious. "But sometimes it isn't. Sometimes it's about a lot more than that. Sometimes it's about the old ways. About life and death and the past and the land. It's about making wrong things right again."

"What are you talking about?" said Ash.

"All those stories my grandfather used to tell. About the land and sacrifice."

"Come on. Those are stories. They're not real."

Mark didn't respond, just crouched in front of Ash and cuffed him on the shoulder. "Sorry I hit you," he said. "You had it coming, though."

"Did I?"

"Yeah, you did," said Mark, the vicious edge creeping back into his voice. "My dad died. Remember that? He was all we had, Callie and me. Then he died and you disappeared. My best friend. You abandoned me."

"It wasn't like that."

"It was exactly like that."

Ash flinched and looked away. "I'm sorry. I didn't know what to do."

"So you ran away."

"Look, I'm sorry. I—"

"And now your dad is back. My dad died but yours came back. Do you think that's fair?"

Ash paused for a moment. "Callie told you about my dad coming home."

"Of course she told me. She's my sister. She's loyal. Not like you. Do you think it's right, that my dad died and yours gets to come home? You're useless and a coward but your dad is fine. I didn't do anything wrong but mine died. Is that fair?"

"Mark. It's not my fault that your dad killed himself."

"I didn't say it was your fault. I asked you if you think it's fair."

"No!" shouted Ash. "Of course I don't think it's fair!"

"See, I've got to make it right again. Whatever it takes, however hard it is."

"Is this why you got Callie to bring me out here? So you could beat me up and even the score?"

Mark's eyes glittered in the firelight. "No," he said. Then

40

his mood seemed to change again. He helped Ash to his feet, draped his arm across Ash's shoulders. "Do you want some water?"

Uneasy, Ash nodded. Mark seemed capable of anything, laughing one minute, punching him the next. Now this.

"Here." Mark handed him a bottle. Ash rinsed blood from his mouth, spat, rinsed again.

"Are you hungry?" Mark asked.

"A little."

"Good." Mark picked up a charred length of stick, crouched by the fire. He raked the stick through the embers and rolled out a heavy lump wrapped in blackened tinfoil. "Venison. Roadkill."

"Roadkill?"

"Yeah. Don't worry, it's fresh, not some maggoty old carcass. A stag hit by a car this morning along the valley road. Its blood was still wet and warm when I found it."

Both boys squatted on their heels, tearing at the meat with their teeth, washing it down with bottled water, sucking their greasy fingers. Ash's jaw ached where Mark had punched him, but at least the strong smoky flavor of the venison took away the taste of blood. For a while, everything seemed almost normal again, the way things were it used to be when they were still kids, camping out on summer nights.

When they'd finished eating, Mark tossed the gnawed bones among the trees. "For the foxes," he said. "Out here, if you take something, you have to give something back. Life for life."

Ash noticed the edge creeping into Mark's voice again, a hint of something savage and raw, as if he'd been in the wild too long, understood it too well. Ash stared into the flames, into the glowing red heart of the fire. "Have you been living out here by yourself all summer?" he said.

"Most of the time, yeah."

"Living on roadkill," said Ash. "And crows."

"I don't eat the crows." Mark laughed. "And it's not just roadkill. I hunt and fish too. There's rabbit and pigeon and berries and trout and mushrooms. My dad taught me how to live off the land. There's all sorts of stuff to eat, if you know where to look."

"Like when we used to go camping."

"Yeah," said Mark. "Kind of like that, except without the soggy cheese-and-tomato sandwiches and hot chocolate. We were kids messing around back then. It's different now."

Ash was quiet for a moment. Mark was right. Everything had changed, was still changing. Nothing seemed solid or certain anymore. Death and disaster could come out of a clear blue sky and rip your life apart. All you could do was hang on and hope.

"I'm sorry about your dad," said Ash. "And I'm sorry I wasn't around much afterward. I should have—"

"Yeah, you should have. But you weren't. When the going got tough, you ran for the hills. You literally ran for the hills and kept running."

"I tried to talk to you."

"Not hard enough."

"I know. I'm sorry." That word again. Ash was sick of saying it but it kept coming out. "I wish everything could go back to the way it used to be."

Mark gave a short laugh, sharp as a fox yelp. "Everything is what it is," he said. "And it's nothing like it used to be."

"I'll make it right somehow," said Ash. "I'll make it up to you."

"My dad's dead. We lost the farm. How will you make that right?"

"That's not what I meant. Of course I can't make that right."

"No, you can't. Only one thing can make that right."

"What, then?"

"The death of the stag boy."

Ash stared at him. "What do you mean?"

"This year. At the Stag Chase. The stag boy has to die. It's the only way to set things right. Life for life."

Ash shifted a little, his nerves on edge. He thought about the strange stag boy he'd seen running in the mountains, the hound boys hungering along his trail. That terrible scream.

"The land's sick," said Mark. "The sickness killed all the sheep. Killed my dad too. Now there's a drought and all the crops in the fields in the valleys are withered and dry. The old ways are coming back."

"What old ways? What are you talking about?" said Ash.

Mark didn't look at him. His voice was soft, trancelike, almost as if he was talking to himself. "The land needs blood. The stag boy's blood. That's the way it used to be in the old days, a sacrifice to the land in a time of need. Well, it's a time of need again, isn't it? The land is dying and there are ghosts rising from its bones, ghosts that kill."

"Come on. You don't believe in those ghost stories. No one believes that stuff, not really."

"I do," said Mark. "More than that. I know it's true. That's why I asked Callie to bring you here. Ash, you have to pull out of the Stag Chase."

"You want me to pull out of the race because of some stupid story about ghosts and the old ways?" said Ash.

Mark bared his teeth—a smile or a snarl. Ash wasn't sure which.

"It's only a race. It's not that big a deal," said Mark.

"It's a big deal to me. No way I'm going to pull out."

"Then you'll die," Mark said.

"Don't be ridiculous. I'm not going to die."

Ash gazed into the fire. The flames were starting to dwindle. A charred branch, bowed like the scorched rib of a giant beast, collapsed. Firefly sparks and flakes of snowy ash drifted skyward. Ash breathed in a lungful of smoke and started to cough. Then he froze, stifling his coughs with his hands.

Someone was watching them.

ASH ONLY CAUGHT A GLIMPSE of him. A face among the shadows, a dark bulk. Then the man turned away and was gone, vanished into the night.

"There's someone here," said Ash. He pointed toward where the man had stood. "Over there, in the trees."

Mark glanced across. "I don't see anyone."

"He was there. I just saw him."

"What did he look like?"

Ash shrugged. "Hard to tell. Big. Wearing dark clothes, I think."

"Was he wearing a hat?"

"I don't know. Maybe."

"Bone Jack," muttered Mark. Scowling, angry again.

"Who?"

"The wild man, the soul-taker."

"The what?"

"It's Bone Jack who guards the boundary between the living and the dead out here. He keeps everything in its place and he takes lives as he sees fit. My dad. The roadkill stag. It makes no difference to him. It could be you next time. It could be me." Mark grinned. "Or maybe I'll beat him. Maybe I'll kill all his birds and take all his power and bring back my dad from the dead."

Ash stared at him. What if Mark was crazy and believed all this stuff he was saying? Sheep skulls, the old ways, human sacrifice, killing crows, this creepy Bone Jack character. Bringing back his dad from the dead.

But another, darker thought played through Ash's mind—that Mark wasn't crazy at all. Ash had seen weird, impossible things with his own eyes lately—the strange stag boy fleeing the hounds, the shadows that had raced behind him along the path, the black feather that seemed to ooze evil. Maybe it was the world that had gone crazy, not Mark.

Ash shivered.

Mark laughed and jabbed at the fire with a stick. "Don't look so worried. You probably saw a poacher, that's all. We're not the only ones out and about in the woods at night."

Ash forced a smile. "Yeah, well, this place is freaky. All those sheep skulls in the trees. Did you do that?"

"Yeah."

"There must be at least a dozen of them," said Ash. "Where did you get them from?"

"They were our sheep," said Mark. "Some of the ones that were slaughtered in the foot-and-mouth outbreak."

"The government sent people to burn the carcasses, and buried them. I was there. I saw it," said Ash. "Did you dig them up and stick their skulls in trees?"

Mark shrugged, looked away. "Maybe."

Ash imagined him out there alone, digging down through the stony soil into the burial pits, hauling out skulls sticky with mud and gore. The thought made him shudder. Maybe Mark had gone crazy after all.

Ash changed the subject. "There was something weird going on up near Stag's Leap the other day," he said. "Hounds chasing a stag boy."

"The Stag Chase isn't for another couple of weeks still."

"Twelve days. I know. That's what was so weird. I saw the whole thing. They ran right past me. Then it was like they vanished into thin air."

Mark shifted. Suddenly he seemed guarded, unreadable.

"Callie was out there too, but she said she didn't see them," Ash continued. "She said you'd know something about it."

Mark looked sideways at Ash. "It's like I told you. The land's dying. Drought, the sheep all slaughtered, my dad swinging on the end of a rope. Shadows in a wasteland, that's what we are, Ash."

"You're not making any sense," said Ash. "All this dark stuff. It's just old legends and ghost stories. You always used to say you didn't believe in stuff like that."

Mark hunched over, rocked himself. "Bone Jack took my dad's life."

"Mark, listen to me. Your dad took his own life."

But Mark didn't answer. He just rocked and rocked. Then he stopped, straightened. "Those boys you saw up on Stag's Leap," he said, "the stag boy and the hounds—they were ghosts."

The pounding of their feet on the parched ground. The stag boy's stumbling run, the exhaustion on his face.

"Come on," said Ash.

"You don't believe in them. I get that," said Mark. "I didn't use to believe in them either. But there *are* ghosts in the mountains. Many of them. You'll see. This land's all blood and bone. All the lost and the dead, they're out here."

"Mark, this is crazy. Do you hear yourself? They weren't ghosts," Ash said, uneasy. "They looked unreal, but that was just the heat haze. It makes everything look like a mirage. They were flesh and blood, like us."

"Flesh-and-blood people don't vanish into thin air."

"What about the boys who were here earlier? The ones who were dancing around the fire? They seemed to vanish, like the hound boys I saw. You're telling me they were ghosts too?"

"You weren't a hound boy last year," Mark said. "If you had been a hound, you'd understand. There's all sorts of rituals and stuff if you're a hound."

"Yeah, I know—the hounds hassling the stag boy, playing pranks."

Mark poked the fire again. The flames guttered and leaped.

"In the old days," he said, "it was serious. The hounds distanced themselves from the stag boy, because if they caught him in the Stag Chase, they had to kill him. It meant he was weak, see. Too weak to outrun them. And if he was weak, then that meant the land was weak and blight would follow. The crops would fail. The animals would get sick and die. There'd be sickness, hunger. Then people would die too. So if the hounds caught the stag boy, they killed him. A blood offering to the land, to make it strong again. A sacrifice. That's bad, isn't it? That's savage. But sometimes you have to do bad things to make other things right. Sometimes you don't have a choice."

The strange stag boy running, desperate, frightened. Running for his life. That final awful scream.

A blood offering.

Was it possible? Was that what Ash had seen on Stag's Leap?

"A sacrifice to what?" Ash asked.

"To the land," Mark said. "It's a bargain with the gods of the land. People have been sacrificing animals and humans to gods for thousands of years, all over the world."

"Yeah, well, so what? Everyone knows those sorts of thing used to happen a long time ago. Torture and witch burnings and human sacrifice and other stuff. It doesn't mean they're happening now."

"Of course not," said Mark. "This is the twenty-first century. We're civilized. We don't sacrifice people these days. When the land is sick, the government sends men in biohazard suits to kill and quarantine everything."

Ash knew Mark had been through a lot. But still.

"Come on," said Ash. "The Stag Chase is just a glorified cross-country race, with costumes and stupid masks and hot dog stands and charity fund-raising and TV crews and tourists."

"Sometimes. But other times, when things get really bad, it's like the ancient days again. It's all blood and darkness. That's why you have to drop out of the Stag Chase."

Ash's mind raced. Something was going on, something out of the ordinary, that he was sure of. But all this talk of ancient times, of blood and darkness and ghosts, seemed too over the top, as if Mark was trying to scare him. And yet . . . Mark sounded deadly serious. Perhaps he was. Perhaps he truly believed what he was saying. "You really think the hounds are going to kill me?" said Ash, still half expecting that Mark would shake his head, laugh, tell him he'd been joking all along.

"Not the hounds," said Mark. "Me."

Ash searched Mark's eyes for something recognizable. He only saw darkness.

"What do you mean . . . you?"

"Life for life," said Mark. "The stag boy's life in exchange for my dad's. I'm going to bring him back, make things right."

Ash just stared.

"I don't want to kill you," Mark went on. "But the stag boy, whoever he is, has to die. That's why you have to pull out of the race. Let some other boy be the stag."

"This is crazy," said Ash. He watched Mark in the fire's glow. "Really crazy. No one is killing anyone. Come down off the mountain with me. We'll talk to my mom. Maybe you can stay with us for a while and we can help you out."

"I don't need any help. I'm exactly where I need to be. It's not like when we were kids, Ash. I'm not going to come home with you and have some dinner and then tomorrow we go off mountain biking somewhere. Those days are gone."

"Callie's worried sick about you. And I am too. Don't you even care?"

"Callie's just a kid."

"You're all she's got left."

50

"She'll be fine. She can look after herself. Besides, I'm doing all this as much for her as for me. We need our dad back. Both of us."

Suddenly Ash felt very tired. "It's late," he said. "Maybe I should go home."

"Still quick to run away, I see."

"Shut your mouth, Mark. I'm so sick of this crap. It's bad enough with Dad at home."

"At least you've still got a dad."

Ash fell silent.

"Go on, then. Don't let me stop you," said Mark.

"I'll come back. Soon. Okay?"

"Whatever. I'll either be here or I won't."

"Do you need anything? Food or blankets?" Ash stood up. Suddenly, his jaw throbbed where Mark had hit him. He felt light-headed, delirious.

As if from a long way off he heard Mark say, "Thanks, but I've got everything I need."

Mark stretched out on the ground next to the fire. Closed his eyes.

Ash walked away. In his mind he heard Mark's voice again, saying, *I don't want to kill you . . . Let some other boy be the stag.*

It would be easy, so easy to let it go, to walk away from the Stag Chase and whatever madness Mark was spinning around it. Let some other boy be the stag. Let everything be that other boy's problem. Then all Ash would have to worry about was Dad.

But Ash couldn't do that, wouldn't do that. He wasn't about to throw away months of training just because a few strange things had happened and Mark was making wild threats.

Ash walked on, into a darkness that stretched from horizon to horizon. A night dusted with stars, crowded with ghosts.

9

THE HOUSE WAS DARK WHEN Ash got home. He walked softly along the driveway. With a bit of luck, he could sneak into the house and upstairs to his bedroom without Mom finding out that he hadn't been in his room all evening.

But as he approached the front door, it swung open and there was Mom. She must have been waiting for him, watching through a window as he came towards the house.

"It's almost midnight," she said ushering him inside and along the hallway to the kitchen. "Where have you been? Why are you out so late?"

"Sorry," he mumbled. He couldn't tell her about Mark. She'd ask too many questions, get involved, and she was anxious enough about Dad as it was.

"What have you been up to?"

"Nothing much," he said. "I went for a walk and it got dark so I lay down to look at the stars and I guess I fell asleep."

"Why did you go for a walk? Were you worrying about Dad?"

"Yeah, a bit. How is he, anyway?"

"Sleeping, I imagine. That's all he seems to have the

energy for since he got home. I took him up some soup earlier. He hadn't touched his lunch."

Ash was quiet for a minute, but he felt uneasy. "What's wrong with him, Mom? Why did he go off drinking for two days instead of coming straight home like he usually does? He looks sick, really sick. And now he's shutting himself up in the spare room and acting strange."

"He's been through a lot. He needs to get his bearings and settle back into civilian life. It's hard but he'll be all right."

"Do you think he has PTSD?"

Mom sighed. "It's crossed my mind."

"So shouldn't we do something? Call a doctor?"

"It's not that simple," she said. "There's already an army counselor waiting to see him, but he won't go and he won't have the counselor come to the house either. He's not ready yet, I guess."

"When will he be ready?"

"I don't know. But he's only been back a couple of days. Maybe once he's adjusted to being home again, he'll be all right."

"What if he isn't?"

"Then we'll deal with it."

"What if we can't?" Ash said.

"We will."

"Yeah, but what if we can't? What's the backup plan? What if we're not enough?"

"It might take some time but we'll get through this," she said. "He's still your dad, the same man who taught you how to ride a bike and pitch a tent and run like the wind. Don't forget that. He's just a bit lost right now."

"What if he stays lost? He might—" But Ash couldn't say it.

"No, he would never do that," his mom said sharply. So sharply that Ash knew she'd had the same thought. That they were both worried he might end up like Mark's dad.

Then she changed the subject. "Not long now until the Stag Chase."

"Yeah, twelve more days."

"Are you ready for it?"

A few days ago, he'd have grinned and told her all about his training. But Mark's warning, full of blood and darkness, cast a shadow over everything.

"I think so," he said. "I hope so anyway."

"You'll be careful, won't you?" his mom said. "The Stag Chase is a tough race. The pressure will be on. Don't let it get to you. Don't do anything dangerous just to win it."

"I won't, Mom."

"Promise?"

"I promise."

"Okay then." She smiled. "You look like you could use some sleep."

"Yeah, it's been a long day. I'm gonna head to bed."

"Good. And Ash?"

He turned back from where he stood in the doorway.

"Everything is going to be fine. Your father too."

Ash nodded. "Night, Mom."

In his room, he lay in his bed as if it was a boat in the silent ocean of night. Tiredness washed over him, and he surrendered to it.

10

A WEEK PASSED, DAYS GLASSY with heat, the nights as thick as tar. Dad closed off in the guest room and Mom restless, spending most of her time in the garden or out visiting friends. It seemed to Ash that life was on hold, all of them adrift on a windless sea, choosing not to look at the storm clouds gathering on the horizon. He ran every day, and every day he asked Dad to join him. But every day Dad said maybe tomorrow. So Ash ran alone, alternating between punishing long runs and shorter, slower runs that kept his muscles loose without tiring him. In between, he slept, he ate, he played computer games, read books, tried to stay focused.

When he ran now, he saw other boys training out in the mountains. They ran in pairs and sometimes in packs. Hound boys. He watched them warily but there didn't seem to be anything strange about them. They were just boys like him, training for the race. Some were boys he'd never seen before, from towns and villages farther out in the mountains. Others he knew from school, boys he'd been friendly with until he'd beaten them in the trials and become the stag boy. Sometimes they passed him, silent, their eyes cold and hostile. Sometimes they ran alongside him for a while, jostled him, veered off laughing. He hated it but he knew the score. The stag boy was always an outcast in the weeks between winning the trials and running in the Stag Chase itself. So Ash kept his gaze on the path ahead, kept running. It was him against them now until after the race.

Twice he saw a distant figure silhouetted against the sky and he was sure it was Mark. Standing above and apart from it all, watching. He remembered Mark's words again and shivered. *I don't want to kill you . . . the stag boy . . . has to die.*

After a week of being hassled by hound boys, Ash started to run a different route—one that took him far away from where the other boys ran, far from the Cullen farm and Stag's Leap. He took the little paths, the ancient paths, and ran north, then northwest, beyond the wide farming valleys and into the wildlands.

He almost tripped over the dog.

It was lying in a hollow between a lumpy boulder and a thorn tree with a twisted trunk. A big dog, with a rough black-and-gray coat matted with dirt and dried blood.

Someone's pet, lost or dumped out here in the mountains, in the middle of nowhere.

Ash crouched beside it. It didn't move, didn't even seem to be breathing. It looked dead but, in case it wasn't, he spoke reassuringly to it. "It's all right, boy," he said. "I won't hurt you."

No reaction. The dog lay there looking like a moth-eaten fur coat that had been dragged through the dirt.

It must have owners somewhere, people who cared about

it, missed it. They were probably out searching for it this very moment, worried sick. Ash pushed his fingers into the thick hair around the dog's neck. He felt for a collar but there wasn't one.

Maybe it was a stray after all, living wild out here, far away from people.

He ran his hands along its body, felt its bones sharp through its heavy coat. Every rib, every vertebra.

Then a low growl rumbled in its throat. Ash snatched away his hand.

Its eyes half opened: light amber in color, a gaze as ancient and wild as the mountains themselves.

Ash drew a sharp breath. "Where did you come from?" he said softly. "How did you end up out here?"

The creature curled its lip as if it wanted to snarl and snap but didn't have the strength.

Then the spell of wildness, of impossible ancientness, broke and its eyes closed. It was just a half-starved feral stray.

Feral or not, he couldn't leave it to die. He rocked back on his heels and thought about what to do. The dog was too big and heavy to carry back through the mountains. He needed help. He stood up, looked all around, listened. They were a long way from the main trails, but sometimes hikers left the beaten track and ventured out here along the little twisting paths.

Not this morning, though.

Out of the corner of his eye, Ash glimpsed movement on the mountainside. Someone else was out here after all. He drew a deep breath, about to call for help, but something wasn't right. The shape was moving too fast and it looked odd, more like a clot of darkness than a human figure, a fluid shadow racing toward them. He squinted into the sun, trying to see what was casting the shadow, but there was only the empty sky and the empty land.

The shadow sped closer, coming straight for Ash. Just as it was about to reach him, he ducked. Then the shadow stopped. It lay over and all around him. He looked up from within its darkness, his heart thudding. Nothing there but the scrub of heather and bracken, the distant peaks.

Nothing that could cast a shadow like this.

Next to him the dog growled softly, a warning.

Suddenly the shadow shook apart, shattering into fragments that morphed into inky, ethereal human figures that fled this way and that.

Then the shadow-figures thinned, dissolved into sunlight until they were gone.

Ash stood up, heart thumping. He scanned the horizon in every direction.

No shadows. And no people around who might have cast them.

Yet he could still sense their presence. Not evil exactly but savage and predatory, lurking out of sight somewhere on the raw, rocky land. And him and the dog out here alone, miles from anywhere, fragile specks of bone and blood and soft flesh.

Ash felt like a mouse waiting for a hawk to strike.

But nothing struck. The shadow-figures were nowhere in sight. If they had ever been there at all.

He scarcely knew anymore what was real and what wasn't. It was as if Mark had filled his mind with nightmares so that now every fleeting shadow, every distant flicker of movement, seemed laden with menace.

Ash switched his attention back to the dog. He took a bottle from his backpack and dribbled water into its mouth. It licked its lips and swallowed. Ash kept on feeding it water until the bottle was empty. By then, the dog's gaze had lost some of its hardness. It still didn't look exactly friendly, though. And it needed a lot more than water. It needed serious help, a vet. Maybe it was already too far gone even for that.

Ash knew his phone wouldn't work out here. He could never get a signal in the mountains beyond Tolley Carn. It was like a black hole for cell phones. He only brought it out with him because Mom insisted. He tried it anyway, just in case. Sure enough, a blue NO SIGNAL message flashed on the screen.

Ash wiped sweat from his face. He thought about his options. He could run back to the village, get Dad. But he was miles out. It would take too long to get home and back again and he couldn't rely on Dad for help anyway, not anymore.

It was all up to him.

His best bet was to reach a road and flag down a car.

"I'm going to get help," he told the dog. "I'll be back soon."

He climbed up onto the higher ground above the path. A couple hundred yards away, he saw a rocky outcrop as tall as a house jutting out from the mountainside. He scrambled up it and stood at its summit. From there he could see for miles. But there was no one in sight, no roads, no buildings, nothing. As if civilization no longer existed.

Ahead, the mountainside dipped down into a wide, deep valley with a straggly thicket of thorn trees running most of its length.

A breath of bluish smoke unwound above the treetops.

Campers, most likely.

They would have to do.

Ash returned to the path and ran down it until a hunch of mountain hid the thorn trees and the path zagged in the wrong direction, away from where the smoke drifted. He abandoned the path and loped across rough terrain, through bracken and gorse, over rocks and humps of gnarly root. Then he was out of the rough, running easily across a slippery stretch of short wiry grass. He splashed across a shallow, sluggish stream and barged his way through a spiky wall of thorn trees onto open ground.

Ahead stood a shepherd's shelter, a small, ancient building with thick stone walls, a turf roof, two deep-set windows hazed with grime. Smoke drifted from a little crooked chimney.

There was a doorway, but in place of a door hung a curtain made of bird skulls and small bones strung together. The breeze clattered them against one another like Halloween wind chimes.

Behind the bone strings, the interior of the shelter was a deep, quiet darkness.

Suddenly, Ash heard a flurry of movement in the trees behind him, harsh cries, beating air.

He turned. Crows—scores of them. They dropped down onto branches, stretched their necks at him. They rattled their night-black feathers, gunmetal beaks open wide, screaming at him with their rough voices.

The dread he'd felt on the mountain when the shadow dropped over him rushed back. He shot a quick glance at the shelter and glimpsed a face through the bone curtain, blurry and dim as a fish moving through murky water. Then, just as quickly, it was gone again.

Ash raced back through the trees the way he had come.

Until a wild-looking man stepped out in front of him.

11

PANIC RUSHED THROUGH ASH. HE didn't stop to think. He just reacted, hurling himself between the trees to get away. Thorns ripped at his clothes, hair, skin. He crashed through twigs and bright green leaves and raced toward the open ground beyond. Then his foot hooked on a loop of bramble and threw him forward. He twisted as he fell and crashed sideways into a tree.

Heavy hands seized his shoulders from behind and wrenched him around. He glimpsed a raggedy coat, a floppy wide-brimmed hat, gray stubble, mad blue eyes. The man looked vaguely familiar, in the way that a stranger who'd asked you for directions a week ago might. But there was no time to think about that now. Ash bucked his body. He threw out a wild kick and felt his foot connect with bone. His fist sank into the thickness of the man's coat.

The man didn't let go. Instead his fingers dug deeper into Ash's shoulders.

"What are you doing here, boy?" he said. His breath smelled like dead leaves. "What are you after, eh?"

"Nothing." Ash's voice came out in a pathetic whisper.

"Liar."

"I came to get help, that's all. I found a dog."

"What dog? I don't see a dog."

"Not here. It's farther up the mountain. It's sick, just lying on the ground like it can't get up."

The man's grip loosened a little bit. "What kind of dog? What's it look like?"

"I don't know what kind. A big dog, black and gray and covered in mud. It's got wild amber eyes and it's really thin. I could feel all its bones. At first I thought it was dead but it's hanging in there. It won't survive much longer, though, unless I get it some help."

"Amber eyes, eh?" The man's hands slid away from Ash's shoulders. Instantly, Ash launched himself along the path.

Something shot past him, a bolt of untidy black like a bird flying parallel to the ground.

The man was in front of him again.

Ash froze, his breath coming in quick panicky gasps. It was impossible. There was no way the man could have gotten in front of him so quickly.

No way.

Ash tried to speak but the words wouldn't come out.

"Don't try running off again," said the man. There was no menace in his voice. There didn't need to be. "Take me to this dog with wild amber eyes. Quick now."

Ash sucked in air.

There was no choice except to do what the man told him. In silence, Ash led the way across the stream to the rough ground beyond. He was shaking so badly his legs barely obeyed him. Get a grip, he told himself. Breathe. Focus.

Talk to him. Get him to like you a bit so maybe he won't kill you.

He forced out the words. "Is that where you live, in that old shelter?"

"Aye."

"I've run out here a few times but I've never seen it before."

The man grunted. "There are lots of things folks don't see." He walked with a long, unhurried stride, the way Ash had seen shepherds walk. Maybe that was all the man really was, a shepherd, still living out in the mountains even though the sheep were long gone.

"My name's Ash," he said. He felt ridiculous, struggling to make small talk with his captor. "I'm from Thornditch. I came out for a run and then I found the dog and went looking for help. I didn't mean to disturb you or to trespass."

"I know who you are," said the man.

Fear flooded through Ash again. He fell silent. How did this man know him?

They reached the path and trekked uphill. The morning sun was hot on Ash's back. Tiny brown birds flitted and chattered in the gorse. A shiny dung beetle blundered across the path.

It all seemed so ordinary.

Except that he was walking with a freak who was wearing a thick coat and a hat on a hot day and who moved with supernatural speed. The man could be a serial killer for all Ash knew, and they were miles from anywhere, anyone. Miles from help. He could be murdered and buried out here and his body would never be found. No one would ever know.

Sweat crawled down his spine.

The dog was exactly as he'd left it only now its eyes were closed again. Ash stared down at it. "We're too late," he said. "It's dead."

The man grunted. "Dead or not, back he'll go."

"Back where?"

"Back with me, where he belongs."

"What do you mean? This is your dog?"

The man shook his head. "Ain't a dog. That's a wolf."

Ash's eyes widened. "A wolf? Did he escape from a zoo or somewhere?"

"No. He's a wild wolf."

"He can't be. There aren't any wild wolves in Britain. Not anymore. Not for hundreds of years."

"I know that. That's why he has to come back with me."

Ash frowned, confused.

The man hunkered down next to the wolf. The wolf didn't move.

Dead, thought Ash. Dead, dead. They were too late.

The man whispered something, singsong words too softly spoken for Ash to catch. The wolf's ears twitched and his eyes flickered open again. The man smiled. He slid his hands along the wolf's body, then under it, and hefted the beast up into his arms.

Ash could have run then. Unnaturally fast though the man was, Ash would surely be able to outrun him now that he had the wolf in his arms.

But he didn't run. He was still afraid but the strange power of the moment held him there. He'd found the wolf by chance, then found this wild-looking man, brought them together, and somehow Ash belonged there too, woven into the mystery of it all, and he couldn't break out of it, not yet.

"Will he be all right?" said Ash.

"Maybe."

"He looks bad. We should get him to a vet."

"No vets up here. Just me," said the man. His eyes narrowed, slits of blue. "He shouldn't be here. Something brought him through, brought him from long ago."

Ash tensed, remembering what Mark had said to him in the woods: *Sometimes it's about the old ways. About life and death and the past and the land.*

The man was watching him. "You know anything about how this wolf got through?"

Ash shook his head. "What do you mean 'through'? I just found him here."

"What about that lad that's been killing crows?"

The three dead crows hanging from a tree at Mark's camp.

Again, Ash shook his head. "I haven't seen anyone killing crows."

Not exactly a lie.

"Well then," said the man. "You'd better go home now, lad."

Now Ash realized why he looked familiar. Remembered where he'd seen him before. The face in the dark, turning away. "You were in the woods last night," he said. The words spilling out before he could stop them. "I saw you."

Something flickered in the man's eyes. Then it was gone again.

"You ain't my business today," he said. "Go home."

He turned his back on Ash and headed back down the path, walking with the same easy stride as before despite the weight of the wolf in his arms.

Ash watched him go until he was out of sight.

Then the spell that had held him broke. He ran all the way home.

When he got there, Dad was screaming.

THE SCREAMS CAME FROM THE living room. Shattered glass glittered on the dark green carpet. A broken mirror hung on the wall above it. An overturned vase spilling flowers and water. The sofa upside down.

The room stank of whiskey.

Ash stood in the doorway, rooted to the spot.

The news was on, the volume turned up loud. Flyblown children stranded on a tiny island of mud in a swirling tide of brown floodwater. The shadow of a helicopter passing over them. A bomb in a marketplace, dozens dead and injured. A dazed woman walking through the carnage. Apples spilled everywhere.

So strange. All those apples among rubble and twisted metal and blood and bodies.

A yelping scream from somewhere in the room, like the cry of a seagull. Then another yelp, and another.

Blood on the carpet, on the coffee table, dark and glossy.

Ash's stomach clenched.

Dad.

Sitting on the floor next to the sofa, knees drawn up to

his chest, one side of his face pressed against the wall, his eyes wide and crazy with terror.

Ash followed the direction of Dad's gaze.

He was staring at a black feather on the floor. A feather like the one Ash had found in his bedroom. Exactly like it.

And no sign of Mom.

"Where's Mom?" Ash asked.

Blood on the carpet, and Mom nowhere in sight.

Ash's head was full of noise: the TV, Dad, the ocean roar of his own blood rushing through his veins. The feather on the floor, shadow pulsing out of it.

How did it get there?

It couldn't be the same feather Ash had dropped in the river. So where had it come from? Why was it in the house with Dad?

Ash forced himself to look away. "Dad! Where's Mom?"

His dad didn't answer, didn't look at him, just kept staring at the feather.

"What have you done?" Ash said. He couldn't catch his breath. The words juddered out, drowning in the racket from the TV.

"Dad!"

The TV spewing noise. Ash hunted for the remote control. Nowhere to be found. He wrenched the TV's plug out of the socket instead. The screen popped and went black.

"Dad!"

Slowly Dad turned to look at him. Red-rimmed eyes. He looked exhausted, like he hadn't slept in weeks.

Ash was shaking, his whole body trembling. "Dad, where's Mom?"

"She's not here." Mumbling, slurring his words.

"Where is she?"

Dad curled up tighter, pressed his forehead to his knees, rocked himself back and forth. Useless.

"Did you hurt her?" said Ash. "Where is she?"

Nothing.

Ash raced into the hallway, yelling for his mom.

Then he heard her voice.

She was upstairs on the landing, leaning out over the banister. He took the stairs two at a time.

Physically she looked all right. There wasn't a mark on her. But he needed her to tell him so he asked anyway.

"I'm okay," she said. "Calm down. I'm fine."

"There's blood," he said. Still breathless, trembling. "There's blood on the living room floor."

She ushered him into her bedroom and closed the door. "Your dad cut his hand, that's all," she said. "It's his blood, not mine."

"How? What happened?"

"I didn't see, but I think he punched the mirror. His hand was still bleeding heavily when I got there but it's not that bad really. The cuts aren't deep. I've put a bandage on it and I don't think he needs stitches."

Ash drew a deep breath and let it out slowly. "I thought he'd hurt you."

"Oh, Ash. He'd never hurt me. Or you. Your father would rather die than hurt either of us."

Ash nodded but he didn't believe her. Dad wasn't himself, wasn't rational. Right now, he seemed capable of anything.

"Why did he flip out like that?" Ash's hands were still shaking. He tried to steady them but he couldn't.

"I don't know," she said. "I went out for a couple of hours. When I got back, the living room was a mess and he was sitting in the middle of it with the TV on full blast and an empty whiskey bottle next to him. I couldn't find the remote control to turn off the TV."

"I pulled out the plug."

"Oh. Good. I didn't think of that. I panicked, I suppose. Anyway, he was bleeding so I ran and got a bandage. Then I came up here to call the doctor."

"Are we taking Dad there now?" asked Ash.

Mom shook her head. "He's in too bad shape. I don't think we could persuade him to leave the house, never mind drive him all the way to Coldbrook. Don't worry. I explained the situation to the doctor and he's agreed to come out and see your dad here."

Just then they heard footsteps on the stairs and then on the landing, slow and heavy. Ash froze. A moment of silence, then the door to the spare room slammed shut.

Mom sighed. "I'd better go down and clean up the living room before the doctor gets here. Will you give me a hand?"

Ash didn't want to. He was still trembling. He wanted to retreat into his room, like Dad, and play computer games and loud music until his brain fried.

But that would have to wait.

They crept past the door to Dad's room and went downstairs. They picked up the vacuum cleaner, a dustpan and brush, a couple of cloths from the cupboard under the stairs. Then they went into the living room.

Ash's gaze went straight to where the black feather lay. But the feather was gone. He scanned the floor for it.

Where was it?

He searched again. Looked under the table, under the overturned sofa. No sign of it.

No one had been in here except Dad. Dad, who'd been staring at the feather, terror written on his face.

Ash's thoughts raced. Another black feather in the house seemed like more than a coincidence. It was a message, a warning with some sort of supernatural force. And Dad had understood that too, felt its power. But where was the feather now? And how had it gotten into the house? Some-one must have brought it and left it in the room with Dad.

Someone else had been here. Who? Who would do this? None of it made sense.

Dad must know, must have seen someone, but Ash couldn't ask him, not right now.

"Come on," said Mom. "You're supposed to be helping."

"Yeah," he said. "Sorry."

He picked up the vase and mopped up the spilled water soaking the carpet. Then he saw it: blood on the window, a smeary handprint where Dad must have pressed against it after he'd punched the mirror.

Ash wiped a cloth over it, but the blood wouldn't come off. He stared at it, puzzled, still too much in a daze about Dad and the black feather to think straight.

Then it hit him.

The bloody print was on the outside.

Someone had stood out there, watching Dad. Someone with blood on his hands.

Ash looked past the handprint, across the lawn to the line of trees beyond. Something stared sightlessly back at him. A sheep skull, wedged in the fork of a branch.

Mark, he thought. The black feather, the bloody handprint, the skull. All this was Mark's work, using Dad to get to Ash, piling on the pressure to make him give up on being the stag boy. It had to be.

Mom was picking up pieces of the broken mirror. "Be right back," said Ash. "I need another cloth." He stumbled past her with the wet cloth still in his hand. Out into the hallway, out through the front door into sunlight. He stood outside the living room window, wiped away the blood on the glass while Mom was still crouched indoors with her back to him. Then he ran across the lawn and yanked the skull from the tree and shoved it deep under the hedge.

Ash closed his eyes, raised his face to the sun. Let sunlight sear through his eyelids, blinding white blankness.

After a few seconds, he opened his eyes. Blinked away the sun's glare.

Mark had been here, freaking out Dad, playing mind games.

Why? A warning, perhaps. A threat. Mark had told Ash not to run in the Stag Chase and he had refused to pull out. Now this.

"Go to hell, Mark Cullen," said Ash, under his breath. "Leave my family alone and go to hell."

THE DOCTOR CAME, SPENT FIVE minutes with Dad, five with Mom, left a small brown bottle of pills on the kitchen table. "Call me if he doesn't improve," he said. Cheery voice, a smile and a wave, then a few seconds later Ash heard the sound of his car grinding down the gravel driveway, and he was gone.

Ash stayed in his room all afternoon, all evening. Mom knocked but he didn't respond and she didn't come in. "I've left some dinner for you out here," she said.

Ash waited until he heard her go downstairs before he opened the door. A plate piled with sandwiches. He wanted to leave them there, some sort of protest against . . . what? Dad. Mom. Everything. But hunger got the better of him.

While he was eating, he thought about the wolf he'd found and the man in the mountains. He thought about what Mark had said to him about the Stag Chase, Bone Jack, sacrifice and the old ways. He thought until his mind spun with it all.

He needed to find out more, much more, if he was ever to understand what was going on.

He went online and searched for *Bone Jack*. There

were only a handful of hits. The first link led to a page on a medical-school website, dedicated to an anatomical skeleton the students had nicknamed Bone Jack.

He kept scrolling down, clicking on link after link until at last one took him to an online encyclopedia entry about folklore and legends.

Bone Jack. An ancient and obscure folkloric figure, particular to the mountainous region around Coldbrook in northern England. Associated with nature, wildness and renewal. Similar folkloric and mythic figures include the Green Man, Lailoken, Myrddin Wyllt, Taliesin and many others. The few early writings that refer to the Bone Jack figure further associate him with the cycle of life and death and with guardianship of the boundary between this world and the Otherworld, attributing him with the ability to shapeshift between human and bird forms—a characteristic that relates to the pre-Christian Celtic belief that the souls of the dead assume bird form to make their journey to Annwn, the Celtic Otherworld.

Ash sighed. As ever on the Internet, every answer only seemed to lead to more questions. Only the name Taliesin was familiar to him, something he'd studied in school, though of course he hadn't paid enough attention and now he couldn't remember what it was. There was nothing to do but follow the links and read.

He read about Taliesin, a sixth-century Welsh bard whose name meant "shining brow" and whose story was part history and part myth—servant to a sorceress called Ceridwen, a shapeshifter, a poet nowadays best remembered for his most famous poem, *The Battle of the Trees*. Ash clicked on another link and read about Lailoken, also from the sixth century, a mad prophet, a wild man who lived deep in the Caledonian Forest and had an affinity with wild creatures. And Myrddin Wyllt, another crazy wild man of the forest, a character some people thought was the original Merlin.

He looked up the Green Man last, and he was the strangest and most ancient figure of them all, leaves and shoots growing from his flesh, a spirit of springtime, rebirth and growth.

Bone Jack had things in common with all of them, Ash could see that. He was a wild man who lived in a wild place and seemed to prefer the company of birds and beasts to that of humans. A shapeshifter. He was the Green Man's dark alter ego in nature's great cycle of life and death and renewal, frightening and dangerous in some primal way that was beyond cruelty and kindness, the way a storm or a hawk or a wolf is dangerous.

Could the wild man he'd met in the mountains be Bone Jack? Ash wondered. The man had seemed to move with unnatural speed, but there could be a rational explanation for that, couldn't there? Perhaps the man hadn't really moved that quickly and it was just Ash's panic that had made it seem so. A man running fast, taking a shortcut through the trees . . . That was possible, wasn't it? Perhaps that was all that had happened and Ash, stumbling in a panic, had just imagined that the man had moved with supernatural speed.

But what if the man really was Bone Jack—wild, ancient, a myth come to life—and what if there really were ghosts in the mountains, spectral hound boys racing across the land?

And then there was Mark, caught up in it all, spinning out of control, threatening Ash, telling him the land needed blood sacrifice, chasing some insane scheme to bring back his father from the Otherworld.

The Otherworld, Annwn. If Bone Jack was real and the guardian of the boundary between life and death, would Mark need to get past him to reach his father? That night in the woods, Mark had talked about killing Bone Jack's crows and taking his power. If Mark was plotting to attack Bone Jack, did Bone Jack know? If he did, he might come after Mark, after all of them.

Ash shook his head, laughed at himself. It was like something out of a book or a movie, not real life.

He shut down the laptop and went to close the curtains. Taped to the windowpane was a scrap of paper with something scrawled on it. Puzzled, Ash pulled it off and read it.

We need to talk. My camp, tomorrow.
Or I'll find you.

Mark. He must have sneaked up here to Ash's room when he'd come to freak out Dad.

"Get lost, Mark," said Ash under his breath. He crumpled the paper into a tiny ball and tossed it into the trash can.

He switched off the light and lay on his back in the dark. He listened. The night was full of little sounds: the tapping of twigs against the window, leaves stirring in the breeze, the distant fluting of an owl. Every sound made Ash's heart race.

Anything might be out there, coming for him through the clammy night.

Another tiny sound, inside the house this time. Then another, and another. Ash lay still, breathing quietly, concentrating. The sounds became distinct actions: a door opening and closing softly, the pad of bare feet along the landing, down the stairs.

There was a long silence. Then the click of the front door shutting.

Ash rolled out of bed and went to the window. The waxing moon hung above Tolley Carn like a bent silver coin.

A shadow slipped through the darkness at the edge of the driveway. Then it moved out into the wash of moonlight at the gate.

Dad.

Ash watched him go through the gate, turn right along the road, vanish into the night. Nothing that way except mountains and a few farms.

No one Dad would visit at this time of night. At least, not that Ash knew of.

Panic raced through him. Dad out in the mountains, disturbed and alone. Anything could happen to him.

Ash switched on his bedside lamp, pulled on his clothes. Briefly he thought about waking Mom. Then he dismissed the idea; she was worried enough already. So he crept through the house, out the front door, loped down the driveway. No sign of Dad, but Ash knew which way he'd gone.

He started to run.

The hot dark prickled against his skin. He ran under a sky full of stars. The moon above the jagged skyline. Silence. Nothing moving in the hedges or fields, no breeze rustling the leaves, not even the distant drone of a car. Only the thump of his feet, his heartbeat, the rhythm of his breath.

He slowed down as he approached the curve in the road. Dad couldn't be far ahead. Ash didn't want to come charging out of the night, scare him.

The road stretched away, silvery gray in the moonlight. No sign of Dad.

Tall hedges on either side, drystone wall farther along the road. No side streets. Nowhere to go except straight.

But Dad wasn't there.

Then Ash remembered that there was a little gate somewhere here, hidden away in the thick cover of dusty leaves. They'd gone that way before, when they used to run together. Dad must have gone through it. There was nowhere else.

Ash found the crease in the hedge where the gate was and pushed through dense foliage. He felt a lash of tingling heat across the back of his hand where it brushed against a nettle.

Beyond the gate, a faint footpath slanted across a scrubby field and on the far side strode a shadowy figure, quick and purposeful.

Dad.

Ash followed.

Through the mountains, black and soft gray like a charcoal sketch, intense here and smudged there. A burned world. The air thick and warm with a nip to it. Moths grazing his skin.

Silence except for his own footfalls. The shrill scolding

of a bird nearby, disturbed by his presence. A thin shriek, some tiny mammal taken by owl or stoat or fox.

Sometimes he saw Dad in the distance. Sometimes he lost sight of him and panicked and hurried and had to stop himself from calling out.

They had wound their way up to Stag's Leap now, rock veined with moonlight, and from where Ash stood, he could see Dad was standing at the edge, the very edge.

Ash was rooted to the spot, watching, his heart racing.

But Dad didn't jump. He pulled something out of his pocket, held it out over the drop, let go. A little dart of shadow spiraling down.

The black feather.

It had to be.

Then Dad turned, came back down the slope to the path. Ash waited in the shadows, then followed again, along a narrow track that hugged the shoulder of the mountain.

Ahead lay the Cullen farm, dark and silent. Dad stopped at the gate, stood there for a while. Then he turned, looked straight toward Ash.

"Home now, then, son?" said Dad. Soft-voiced, gentle. Like the way he used to speak sometimes, before his last tour of duty, before the PTSD.

Dad must have known he was there all along. Ash walked along the track toward him.

"Yeah."

They walked on for a while.

"I saw you, up on the Leap," said Ash. "You dropped something over the edge. What was it?"

Dad didn't answer.

"Why did you come out here, Dad?"

Dad drew a long breath, let it out slowly. "Tom Cullen was my best friend when we were boys. Like you and Mark. We used to go hunting, fishing, climbing. Not so much later on, though. Him with the farm, me with the army. Marriage, kids, all that. Time passes. And now he's dead."

"It's not your fault."

"Isn't it? I could have been a better friend to him. I could have kept in touch, spent time with him when I was home on leave. I meant to. But I never got around to it and now it's too late."

"You couldn't have known."

"That's it, though. I *should* have known. Him out here on his own after Ella died, two kids to raise and a farm to run. Then there was the foot-and-mouth outbreak, his stock slaughtered." Dad sighed. "I suppose he'd used up all his strength by then. No reserves left. I should have been here. I should have done something."

"You were overseas," said Ash. "You were fighting a war."

Dad looked toward the horizon. Paused. "People keep dying all around me," he said. "And I keep surviving."

They walked on in silence until finally Ash spoke.

"That thing you dropped from the Leap," he said. "I know what it was."

"You do?"

"Yeah, I do. It was the black feather that was on the floor in the living room."

Dad looked at Ash. Sharp and hard. "How did you know?"

82

Ash shrugged. "Just a guess. I saw you—you were staring at it, then it disappeared with you when you left the room. Where did it come from?"

"A bird, I suppose."

"Ha-ha. At least you're still making lame jokes."

Dad grunted. "All I'm good for these days."

Ash gave a small smile.

"It reminded me of something from a long time ago. Stupid, really."

"What?" Ash asked.

Dad shrugged, sighed, shut down.

"How did it get in the house?" said Ash. Pushing, not letting Dad retreat into another of his silences. "Who brought it in?"

"I don't know," said Dad. "There was someone else there. I saw him but I don't know who he was. A face like a skull at the window. Hands dripping with blood." He stopped, ran his fingers through his hair. "I thought it was . . . someone or something that came back with me from the desert, something vengeful. Haunting me. I see them sometimes, in my dreams. The dead. Then there was that feather and . . . maybe I'm . . ."

Breaking down, falling apart again.

"What?"

"I don't know. Hallucinating, or something."

"You're not," said Ash. "It wasn't anything to do with the war. It was Mark, trying to scare me."

But Dad scarcely seemed to hear him. "I saw a feather like that once before," Dad went on. "Years ago, long before you were born, I trained for the Stag Chase out here. And one day a bird flew into me, a crow, I think. I don't know why but it freaked me out. Then the next morning I woke up and there was a black feather on the pillow next to me. It must have gotten caught in my hair, that's all. But still."

Suddenly Ash's mouth felt dry. Dad's description of the bird flying into him all those years ago almost exactly matched Ash's own experience a few days back. It could be a coincidence, thought Ash, but what were the chances?

"You were all right, though?" said Ash. "Nothing bad happened?"

"No, but it almost did."

"What?"

"It was a couple of weeks later, during the Stag Chase. I was the stag boy and I took a route along the length of Stag's Leap. Then I must have zoned out because suddenly I found myself standing at the very edge of the Leap, looking down. I don't even know how I got there. And my body wanted to launch into the air, to jump. It was such a powerful urge I can feel it even now, just thinking about it. Crazy. So I was standing there, sort of frozen between wanting to jump and knowing I shouldn't, and this dread that my body might do it anyway without my permission. And I wasn't alone. I thought I could see these other boys there, like shadows, only in color. They were angry, full of hate. Throwing darkness at me. Trying to force me off the edge."

"But you didn't let them. You were okay."

"I was okay because Tom Cullen saw me standing there, all freaked out. He grabbed me and hauled me back from the edge. He saved my life. He really did. Then he just ran off and left me to finish the race. So I did. And I won. Except I didn't really win, did I, because Tom had caught up with me and then let me go. I told the organizers but Tom denied it. He never did admit to it. Told me I'd gotten mountain fever or something and that I'd imagined it all."

Dad looked straight ahead, his expression hidden by the dark.

They walked on in silence. Ash's mind reeled with what his dad had told him. The bird flying into him, the phantom boys trying to push him over the edge of Stag's Leap, all of it echoed the strange things Ash had experienced lately. And he still hadn't told Dad that he would be the stag boy in this year's race. For a moment, he considered telling him now. But Dad was talking to him at last and Ash didn't want him to stop, didn't want to put himself at the center of the conversation.

And maybe he should take Dad's experience as a warning, a sign that there really were dark forces at work in the mountains, just like Mark said—vengeful wraiths set on killing stag boys. Perhaps he should take it all more seriously and do what Mark wanted, pull out of the race, stay at home, stay safe.

So no, there was no point telling Dad anything yet, Ash thought. Not until he had made up his mind.

"Strange things happen sometimes," he said.

"Yeah, I suppose they do," said Dad. "When I was out in the desert, I kept coming back to that day up on Stag's Leap. I don't know why. I hadn't thought about it in years, then suddenly I couldn't get it out of my mind. Seems like every-where I go I'm surrounded by angry ghosts. They came for me all those years ago and now they're coming for me again."

"But we'll be all right." Ash paused. "Won't we? We'll get through all this."

"I hope so."

Then Dad fell silent again and they crossed the fields in cold moonlight. Half-formed questions drifted through Ash's mind but he was too tired now to ask them. His eyes half closed. Feet dragging. He yawned, longed for his bed and sleep. Dad put his arm around his shoulders and they trudged home, side by side.

IT WAS DAYLIGHT WHEN ASH woke. He checked the alarm clock. It was past nine already. He'd been up too late last night trailing Dad around the mountains and now he'd overslept, messed up his training schedule for the day. He rolled out of bed, pulled on his clothes, hurtled down the stairs two at a time.

Ash stopped in his tracks in the kitchen doorway. Dad was in there, sitting at the table. Fully dressed, clean-shaven, eating scrambled eggs and toast. A fresh bandage on his injured hand. He still looked thin and tired but otherwise he seemed almost like his old self.

"Morning," said Dad. "Do you want some breakfast? I can make more scrambled eggs if you'd like."

Ash was scared to reply in case his words broke whatever spell had brought Dad back to life. "Yeah," he said at last. "Thanks." He glanced across the kitchen. Next to the back door stood a small backpack and a couple of fishing rods sheathed in canvas.

Dad saw him looking and smiled. "I thought we could go out fishing today," he said. "Unless you've got other plans."

Mark's note, summoning Ash to his camp in the wood, ran through his mind. *Or I'll find you.*

Ash hesitated for a heartbeat. "No," he said. "I mean, no, I don't have any other plans. Fishing sounds great." He sat down opposite Dad. "Where's Mom? Is she up yet?"

"Yeah. She's out already. Visiting Harry, I think."

Harry, short for Harriet. Mom's closest friend in Thornditch, a booming woman in her sixties who lived in a tumbledown cottage at the other end of the village.

"I'm amazed she hasn't come over since you got back," said Ash.

"She probably has," said Dad. "I heard Mr. King stop by yesterday morning. Mom sent him away. I don't think I'm allowed visitors at the moment. Probably for the best."

"I thought Mom would be here with you," said Ash. "Now that you're up and about."

Dad gave a wry smile. "I think she's had enough of me lately."

They finished their breakfasts quietly. Dad made a stack of messy ham sandwiches, filled a thermos with coffee and a plastic bottle with tap water. Ash loaded everything into the backpack. He'd worry about his training—and Mark—later.

"Pike Tarn all right?" said Dad.

The other side of Tolley Carn Peak, and where they used to go when Ash was a kid. A cold clear mountain lake, sunlight burning through mist rising from the water, the eerie calls of curlews. "Yeah," said Ash. "Pike Tarn would be good."

They set off.

Sun beat off the ground. Where the road hooked around the ruins of an ancient barn, they stopped to stare at the leathery remains of a frog, flattened by a passing car and sun-dried to a perfect cutout version of itself.

"You tried to eat one of those once," said Dad.

Ash laughed. "No I didn't."

"You did. You were about two, I think. You peeled it right off the road and your mom got it away from you just before you started chewing on it like a piece of licorice."

"Ugh," said Ash. "Gross. Glad I don't remember that."

"Do you remember the last time we came out here?" said Dad. "When we slept out under the stars."

"Yeah," said Ash. He laughed again. "We didn't bring any food with us because you said we'd catch our own dinner. But we didn't catch anything."

"I'd forgotten about that part."

"You had to mooch food off those campers."

"Baked beans and pasta. Delicious!" Dad said.

"We were so hungry by then, even a squashed frog would have tasted good."

Dad smiled. Neither one mentioned last night, the long walk up to Stag's Leap and the Cullen farm and back.

They left the road and followed the footpath past a row of wind-twisted thorn trees up the lower slopes of Tolley Carn. Then, in the valley below, there was a wink of dazzling light.

Dad flinched and shouted out. He grabbed Ash's wrist, hauled him behind the cover of the nearest thorn tree, pushed him down to the ground.

They crouched there.

The seesaw of Dad's breathing, quick and raw.

"What?" said Ash. Dad was trembling, couldn't stop. "What is it?"

Dad's breathing slowed, steadied. He gave a sharp laugh.

Shook his head. "That flash of light down in the valley," he said.

"Yeah," said Ash. "I saw it. It was probably just sunlight catching a car-door mirror or a window."

"No. I know what it was."

Ash watched him.

"There were snipers," said Dad. "Out in the desert. They'd lie in wait in the dunes or on the rooftops of buildings along the roads. Sometimes the sunlight would flash off their rifle scopes. You learn to dive for cover when you see that. Gets to be second nature after a while."

"It's okay," said Ash. "There aren't any snipers here."

"I know," said Dad. He rubbed his hand over his face, drew a long breath. "I know that. Sorry, son."

They stood up, continued along the path. The moment should have passed but it hung on, Dad still on edge, his face glossy with sweat, his eyes scanning the mountainside as if he still half expected snipers to be hiding in the bracken.

"You all right now?" said Ash.

No reply.

Change the subject. Get Dad thinking about something other than snipers and war. But he only had one piece of real news: The Stag Chase. Suddenly Ash's mouth felt dry. After last night, the timing seemed all wrong. But he'd find out sooner or later, and it seemed better if the news came from Ash himself. Dad was up and about now, and in a small place like Thornditch, nothing stayed secret for long.

"I'm running in this year's Stag Chase," he said, the words racing out. "I won the trials last month. I'm supposed to be the stag boy. It's official."

Silence.

"Dad?"

Nothing. It was as if Ash hadn't spoken.

"Dad? Did you hear what I said?"

"Yeah, I heard," said Dad. A taut smile on his face. "That's wonderful news. I'm proud of you."

"You don't mind? Last night . . ."

"Don't worry about what I said last night. My head's all over the place lately. I knew you were going out running every day and I knew the Stag Chase was coming up, but I've been so caught up in my own problems, I never put two and two together. I'm really sorry. You're a great runner. You'll leave them in the dust."

"But what you said, about when you were the stag boy. About wanting to jump off the edge of the Leap and Tom Cullen saving your life. Maybe it's a bad idea. Maybe I shouldn't run."

"That was twenty years ago," said Dad. "Twenty Stag Chases ago. There are always stories about strange goings-on at the Stag Chase. A bit like Halloween, I suppose."

"But you said you saw things yourself out there on the Leap when you were the stag boy. Shadowy figures, ghosts. That black feather."

"Yeah, well, like I said, it was a long time ago. I've seen a lot more since then, good things and terrible things. And right now what I'd most like to see is you out there, running like the wind." He smiled. "Maybe you can put the ghosts to rest for me."

Ash hesitated. Until a few days ago he'd felt proud that

he would be the stag boy but he didn't feel that way anymore. Now he only felt anxious, hemmed in by darkness and danger, everything sliding out of control. But he didn't want to let Dad down. He'd have to go through with it now.

Ash forced a smile. "I'll try. Will you come, then, watch the race?"

"Of course I will."

They trudged up the last stretch to the summit, a crown of burned grass studded with rough gray rock. Beyond, the land fell away steeply to the eastern shore of Pike Tarn.

Dad stopped at the top of the path. He shrugged off the backpack. Then he stood there, staring wide-eyed at the lake as if the mouth of hell had just yawned open before him. Suddenly he was sweating and tense again.

"Dad," said Ash. "What's wrong?"

No answer.

"Dad?"

"Shut up," said Dad. Taking quick, shallow breaths. Still staring toward the lake.

Ash followed his gaze. No flash of sunlight this time. Nothing out there except a crow flapping over the lake toward them, rough cries grating from its open beak.

"What is it, Dad? Is it the bird? The crow?"

And it must have been, because there was only the bird, feathers black and glossy as oil, and Dad's gaze fixed on it as it flew closer.

The crow arced above them, veered away.

"I can't do this," said Dad. "I'm sorry. I'm not ready."

He pushed past Ash, set off back down the path at a stumbling run.

Ash took off after him. "Wait! Dad! What's wrong?"

"Nothing," said Dad. Breathing hard, his eyes full of panic and a strange sort of anger. "Everything. Home. I need to go home."

Ash followed. Words tumbled from him. "Dad, stop. We're here, Dad, on Tolley Carn. It's all right. The lake's just over there. We'll go down and do some fishing like we planned. Dad! Please. It's okay."

Dad's voice came back to him, raw and desperate. "Leave me alone, Ash. Stop following me!"

Ash stopped. He watched his dad go, running and stumbling back along to the road until he was lost to the distance.

Ash crouched in a patch of shade thrown by a thorn tree. Head in his hands, blinking away tears. He felt sick inside. The last thing he wanted to do now was trail back along the path in Dad's wake to the silent house, the closed doors, the tension that never seemed to go away.

He stood up. There was still the whole day ahead of him. Briefly he thought about going to Mark's camp, like Mark wanted him to. But he was tired of dealing with it all, with the strangeness and shadows that now seemed to haunt his every move, his every thought, with Mark, with Dad.

Ash walked back to the summit and picked up the backpack and fishing rods where Dad had dropped them.

On the far shore of the lake, there were boys diving from the rocks. Their distant voices and laughter echoed across the water. Careless, carefree. Kids from school, most likely, but they were too far away for him to see their faces. A year ago, he and Mark might have been with them, diving down into the deep dark water until their lungs felt about to burst, then kicking upward again toward the bright shimmer of sunlight on the surface.

A sudden loneliness hollowed Ash. He didn't make friends easily. He was too skinny and too intense, the sort of kid bullies gravitate toward. Not a fighter like Dad. Or like Mark. But Mark had always been there, ever since Ash could remember, and no one messed with Mark so no one messed with Ash either, so long as Mark was around. But now Mark was gone to the wild, and none of the other boys would hang out with Ash until after the Stag Chase.

Ash had no one. There was nothing to hold on to anymore except the Stag Chase, and even that felt like it was slipping away from him, with its dark history unfolding.

He slithered untidily down the steep slope. His feet loosened a mini-landslide of stones that bounced down ahead of him, but the diving boys were too far off to notice.

On the narrow shingle beach that bracketed the lake he took off the backpack, set it on the ground, and stripped down to his boxers. He waded in, then swam out and floated on his back.

Swallows skimmed the water for insects.

Underneath him stretched the great depth of lake and landscape, the earth turning under cloudless heights of sky.

And Ash was just a speck drifting, shoreless.

ASH SAT ON A ROCK and let the sun dry his skin and hair. He watched the distant boys messing around at the water's edge. He ate some of the sandwiches Dad had made, washed them down with bottled water. Then he pulled on his shorts, his walking boots and T-shirt, hooked the backpack over his shoulders and scrambled back up the slope to the top of Tolley Carn.

Below him to the east lay Thornditch.

To the south, Carrog Ridge and beyond that the road that ran around to the Monks Bridge and then toward Mark's camp.

High on Carrog Ridge Ash saw a solitary figure standing motionless, silhouetted against the pale sky.

The figure lifted one arm, waved, gestured as if it wanted him to come across.

The hairs on the back of Ash's neck prickled. He knew it wasn't Dad. Dad would be at home by now, shut in his dark room again.

Or I'll find you, Mark had said in his note.

It had to be him.

For a moment, Ash hesitated. He could walk away, keep

his head down, focus on his running for the last few days before the Stag Chase.

But he needed more answers, and Mark was the only one who could give them.

Ash set off toward the ridge.

Just then the crow returned from the other side of the lake, a black rag flapping across a pale sky. Its soft honking call sounded above him for a while, then the bird flew off. Just a regular bird. Nothing sinister, nothing mysterious.

Mark was still there on the high ground, still watching Ash when he came to the narrow valley on the southern side of Tolley Carn. Mark raised his arm again and pointed in the direction of his woodland camp. Then he dropped down below the skyline, out of sight.

Ash left the path and walked through knee-high grass as dry as tinder. Butterflies flopped in the windless air. A pair of buzzards circled lazily high above him. He reached the road and followed it around the foot of Carrog Ridge to the Monks Bridge and beyond. Then he took the route Callie had shown him to the woods where Mark was camped.

Ash stepped from the hot glare of sunlight into cool shadow.

The bone faces watched him with their sightless eyes.

Around them, the woods were gloomy and silent. No sign of Mark anywhere, except for the sheep skulls.

Somewhere above the leaf canopy, a buzzard mewed.

The campfire in the clearing was a patch of cold white ash and a few charred sticks. Around it, the tall grass and nettles were broken and crushed as if a dozen or more people had trampled through.

There was something else too. A trace of wood smoke in the air. The iron stink of blood.

He looked down.

Rusty flecks spattered on grass and fern. A small pool of blood on the ground, blackish red and glossy. He crouched, touched the tip of his forefinger to its surface.

It was still tacky.

Whether it was animal or human blood, Ash couldn't tell. Either seemed possible.

He remembered the venison Mark had cooked on the fire. Maybe that's all it was, blood spilled from another gutted deer.

He crossed the clearing.

A breeze stirred the leaves.

Now he could smell more than just blood and wood smoke. A sickly sweet, rotten stench filled the air. Flies and wasps stormed under the trees. He swatted them away.

He looked around. Nothing.

Then he looked up.

A stag carcass hung from a branch above, swinging in the breeze. Its head was gone, hacked off. Maggots bulged and gleamed in the blackened gore at its neck.

Ash covered his nose and mouth with one hand, tried not to breathe. His stomach heaved.

There was a movement in the bushes beyond the carcass. A flash of white and red. Laughter.

"Ash," called a voice. As soft as the breeze through the leaves. "Over here!"

"Mark," said Ash. Heart thumping. "Stop messing around."

More laughter.

"Over here," said the voice. Louder this time.

Ash turned.

A figure came through the trees. Sackcloth mask, scabby with dried clay. Ragged mouth, eyeholes that seemed to have only shadows behind them.

Not tall enough to be Mark.

Now more hound boys approached behind the first. Ash turned to run but they were all around him, coming from all sides, closing in.

No way out.

Mark had lured him into a trap.

The hound boys came closer. Their dry, clay-crusted skin pressed against him. The scent of blood came from them, hot and metallic. Their whispering voices were as scratchy as the wind in dead grass, and as senseless. Ash couldn't tell if they were flesh and blood or the strange otherworldly runners he'd seen up on the Leap nearly a week and a half ago.

They wrenched the backpack from his shoulders.

That felt real enough.

"Hey, that's mine," he said. He grabbed at it, missed. "Give it here!"

Boys from school, he thought. Boys tormenting him because he was the stag boy, and because Mark had put them up to it. They'd rough him up a bit, try to scare him.

It was working. Ash couldn't catch his breath. His heart raced with fear.

The hound boys laughed behind their masks. They

passed the backpack from one to the next, through their ranks and closed in tighter.

One of them scooped up a handful of ash from the cold remains of the campfire. He threw it in Ash's face, rubbed it into his skin and hair. Ash coughed and choked, eyes streaming.

They surged forward and the weight of their bodies bore him along with them. They hauled him over a fallen tree poxy with black fungus, across ground ankle deep with ivy, past clumps of bracken and green licks of hart's tongue.

Smoke from a small fire drifted under the leaf canopy. The hounds stopped, gazed into its bright heart. One of them tossed a handful of something into the flames. The smell of burning leaves. Ash's eyes, nose, throat filled with bitter smoke.

They seized him, pushed him to the ground. Held down his arms and legs so he couldn't move.

"Be still," hissed one. "Be still for the stag god."

At first, Ash only saw a silhouette, a shadow. The afternoon sunlight slanted through the trees behind him, hazy beams, dust motes drifting and sparkling. Then he saw that the god was taller than any of the hound boys. A cloak of black feathers swung about him. Instead of a man's head, a stag's head sat upon his shoulders, crowned with spreading antlers.

The hounds drew back to let him through.

Ash stared up into two dull, dead eyes. The stag's nose and half-open mouth clotted with congealed blood.

The stag god crouched over him. The stench of blood, rotten meat, death.

And the cloak. It was made of bird skins, feathered and bloody, eyeless heads still attached. Steely beaks.

Crows, like the dead crows Ash had seen hanging from a branch the last time he'd come here.

The stag god took a thin, vicious knife from under his cloak. The hand that held it was caked with cracked clay, the color of rust or dried blood. Black dirt under his fingernails.

"Earth and stone," whispered the stag god, "fire and ash, blood and bone."

"Mark," said Ash. His voice shaking. "I know it's you."

"Be still. It will hurt less if you're still."

"What will hurt less?" Ash tensed, tried to wrench away from the hounds pressing down on him. But there were too many of them, too strong, too heavy. He couldn't catch his breath. Maybe Mark wasn't going to wait for the Stag Chase. Maybe this was it—the kill, the blood sacrifice that he had threatened. "Killing me won't bring back your dad," Ash said. His voice thin and shaky.

"*Hush!* Be still!"

The knife descended tip first. Ash felt its cold bite as it broke the skin below his collarbone. He flinched, bit back a cry. The hounds whooped and hollered and bayed. Then the cold became a white-hot thread of pain that moved this way and that across his chest.

The stag's dead eyes watched without seeing. Ash gazed back through a haze of pain and smoke and blood and terror. A cloud of flies buzzed around the rotting head. Then the knife lifted, vanished back under the cloak of bird skins. Mark straightened and stood. He raised his head and bellowed. Then he turned away from Ash, walked off through the hound boys, disappeared into the gloom.

Ash sucked in air. A knot of darkness unraveled inside him. The world around him spun away, dimmed and disappeared.

When he opened his eyes again, he was alone.

Ash sat up. Pain clawed across his chest. Wincing, he got to his feet. His stomach heaved. Bile flooded his mouth. He gagged and spat.

The wood was silent except for the shrill staccato jabber of a startled blackbird.

The fishing rods and the backpack were on the ground where the hounds had dropped them. Ash rummaged through the backpack and found the water bottle, rinsed his mouth, spat, then drank deeply.

A tiny sound, the pop of a twig cracking underfoot.

He looked up.

In the darkness among the trees a shard of sunlight lit up a face. Someone standing there, watching. For a heartbeat, Ash saw his face clearly. He'd seen him before, talked to him.

It was the wild man who'd taken the wolf.

Then, before he realized what was happening, the breeze scattered leaf shadows and the sunlight broke apart into more shadows that became the beating black wings of birds—crows that rasped and cawed and shrieked as they rioted up through the treetops and away into the sky.

Bone Jack.

It had to be.

Fear washed through Ash again. He grabbed the backpack and ran. He didn't stop running until he got home.

16

ASH STOOD AMONG THE TREES at the end of the driveway. He stared up at the house. Most likely Mom was in the back garden but he couldn't count on it. He couldn't let her see him, not pale with ash, his shirt slashed open and his chest all cut up and bloody.

Hidden in the undergrowth, he waited. He watched the house until he was certain Mom wasn't inside and Dad was holed up in his room. Then he loped to the front door and let himself in.

Silence.

Upstairs, he locked the bathroom door behind him. He stood in front of the mirror. Dried blood crusted his chest.

His face was ghostly with the ash the hound boy had thrown at him.

He soaked a washcloth in cold water and squeezed it out over the wounds on his chest, wiped away blood, rinsed the cloth, wiped away more blood.

He looked in the mirror again. Now that most of the blood was gone, a pattern was visible: a crude stag's head cut into his flesh, just like the one he'd seen daubed on the stag boy's chest that day on the Leap.

Ash drew a sharp breath. He ran his fingertips over the cuts. The wounds were tender and shallow, not much more than scratches. The knife tip had broken the skin but not gone deeper. They'd hurt for a few days and then they'd heal, probably not even leave a scar.

Even so, terror hammered in his chest.

Ash took slow breaths, tried to calm himself down but his heart kept pounding and his mind raced. There had to be an explanation for it all. The stag god wasn't any sort of god. It was just Mark, wearing a grotesque headdress made of the dead stag's head and a cloak made from bloodied bird skins. Horrific and crazy, but still Mark. And the hound boys were just ordinary boys behind their masks, doing what Mark told them. Somehow Mark had made himself their leader. Because he was cleverer, quicker, stronger, wilder, more charismatic than they were. Because he was mad and his madness made him powerful.

Just boys. It was all just boys. Nothing supernatural. They were playing mind games, trying to intimidate Ash. The hounds always intimidated the stag boy before the race, he reminded himself. It was expected.

Everything was all right.

But it didn't feel all right. It felt dark, dangerous. There was death all around. The stag's head, all those crows. Mark must have caught them somehow, maybe netted them or shot them down with a catapult. And then he'd killed them, skinned them, made them into that cloak. It was sick, wrong.

And Bone Jack watching from among the trees. Always

at the edge of things, and yet at the heart of them at the same time. Connected to everything, following his own agenda. But what *was* his agenda? What did he want? Mark thought he was in control but Ash knew what Bone Jack could do, he'd seen it, and there was no way Mark was calling the shots.

Ash wished he could talk to Dad about it all, ask him if he knew what all this stuff meant, ask him what he should do. But Dad was lost in his own nightmares. He couldn't handle Ash's terrors as well.

Ash's head ached with it all.

He showered, washed away the last traces of blood and the bitter smell of smoke that clung to his skin and hair. He found the first-aid kit that Mom kept in the bathroom cabinet. He smeared antiseptic cream over the wounds and taped bandages over the top. Then he wrapped himself in a huge towel and crept upstairs to his bedroom on the top floor. Still no sign of Mom or Dad anywhere. He stuffed the bloodied T-shirt and washcloth into a corner at the back of the closet, and dressed himself in clean clothes.

Everything hidden and as ordinary as he could make it.

Ash lay on his bed. Sunlight played across the ceiling. His body felt empty, a shell. He floated above it, half asleep, far away from everything. Dad, his head full of demons. Mom trying to cope, acting as if things were okay even though she and Ash both knew they weren't.

Lies. Secrets. Blood and death. None of it made any sense. Ash wasn't sure anymore if the world had gone mad or if he had.

He turned his head, gazed out the window. Unblinking.

He needed to find Callie. She was the only person he could think of who might understand any of this. The only person who might know what Mark was doing and might be able to make him stop.

Tomorrow, though.

It would have to wait until tomorrow.

He was weary to the bone. Ash closed his eyes and let sleep take him.

NEXT MORNING ASH DRESSED IN his running gear. He walked to the main street and caught the bus to Coldbrook. He didn't have much of a plan in mind. Find Callie and talk to her. Return home on foot, walking and running, a last training session before winding down and taking it easy for the next two days until the Stag Chase.

A couple of boys from his year at school were horsing around at the back of the bus. Liam Tunney and Chris Brooker. They shot glances at him. They whispered and snickered. "Dead man walking," said Brooker loudly. They both laughed.

Ash stayed away from them. He sat near the front, among the old folks and other passengers on their way to Coldbrook's shops and cafés. He felt the boys' eyes on him, heard their voices and laughter but he didn't look around. They were hound boys, he knew. Almost every local youth between the ages of thirteen and sixteen would be a hound boy in the Stag Chase. So they'd probably been there yesterday too, in the woods with the other boys, their faces hidden behind masks, holding Ash down while Mark carved the stag's head into Ash's chest.

He wondered how much else they knew. They could be

in on everything, part of Mark's plan to kill the stag boy and bring back his dad from the dead.

Ash pushed the thought aside. He told himself he was just being paranoid.

Beyond the window, the trees lining the road gave way to drystone walls and patchwork fields, then the rough open moors of the uplands. The bus crested a hill and now Coldbrook filled the valley below, a sprawl of tightly packed houses rising in tiers up the lower slopes of the mountains to either side.

One of those houses belonged to Grandpa Cullen.

Ash had been there once before, with Mark. But that was a long time ago and all Ash remembered was a few worn steps leading from the pavement to a green front door. A whitewashed terraced house. A curve of railing. A fiery orange geranium in a flowerpot.

Where, though? The only parts of town Ash knew well were the main street and the bus route to his school. But there were so many other streets, so many houses. They all looked alike.

He got off the bus in the town center. Liam Tunney and Chris Brooker got off too. They cackled like hyenas and elbowed each other as they passed him. Ash hung back, watched them head off along the street until they disappeared into the crowd.

Cars, shoppers, music blaring from a clothing shop, a streak of kids pelting past on BMX bikes. The rush of noise and movement made him giddy. He walked along until the street split into three at a traffic circle. Then he walked back again, wandered down a cobbled side street that swung sharply to the left before it ended abruptly at a high brick wall mottled and veined with faded blue graffiti.

Ash tried to retrace his steps to the main street. He stopped at a corner, turned this way and then that, wondering what to do, where to go. Without the name of the road Grandpa Cullen lived on, he couldn't even ask for directions or look at a map. He had no idea where he was.

"You look lost, dear," said a voice. Two elderly women, smiling kindly at him. They both looked old enough to have been at school with Grandpa Cullen.

"I'm looking for my friend's grandpa's house," he said. "Only I can't remember where it is."

"What's his name?" said one of the women. "Maybe we know him."

"Cullen," said Ash. "Mr. Cullen."

"George Cullen," said the first woman, looking at the other. "He must mean George Cullen."

"Pocket Lane, I think," said the second. "Is that right? Or is it Harper Lane?"

"Pocket Lane," said the other. "Definitely Pocket Lane." They directed Ash toward the north side of town. Third row of houses beyond the church spire, or was it the fourth row? Somewhere around there anyway.

"I'm not sure about the house number, though," said the first woman. "You'll have to ask someone else when you get there."

"I will," said Ash. "Thanks."

Pocket Lane. He recognized it as soon as he saw it,

though it was narrower than he remembered and the houses were smaller and grubbier. Grandpa Cullen's whitewashed house stood out among the dark gray stone and pebbledash. There were the steps up to it, the railing, the green door. Only the potted geranium was gone. The windows were dark.

Ash rang the doorbell and waited.

Nothing.

He rang it a second time, then hammered the brass knocker for good measure. Still nothing. He leaned over the railing and peered through the living room window. No one there, just a fireplace, a couple of heavy old armchairs, a coffee table with a folded newspaper and a stack of unopened letters on top of it, a TV set in the far corner. He drew back and knocked on the front door again.

A neighbor came out from next door. A large middle-aged woman with honey-colored hair, her rolled sleeves exposing powerful forearms. A cold, suspicious expression on her heavy face. "Can I help you?" she said.

"Is this where George Cullen lives?" he said.

Her eyes narrowed. "What do you want with Mr. Cullen?"

"It's not him exactly. I'm looking for Callie, his granddaughter."

"What do you want with Callie, then?"

"It's personal."

She stared at Ash, stone-faced.

"I want to talk to her about her brother," he said. "Mark. I know him from school. He was my best friend."

"Was?"

"We had a falling-out."

"Ah. And now you want to make up with him, do you?" The woman's expression softened a little. "They're not here, love."

"It's okay. I'll wait."

"They're not coming back. No one lives here now. George fell sick and has been in the hospital for about a month now. He couldn't look after himself, never mind take care of two children. Not that it was much of a surprise. His health has been declining for years. I don't suppose he'll last much longer, bless him."

Ash stared at her, shocked. If their grandpa had been in the hospital, Mark and Callie were even worse off—and more alone—than he'd realized.

The neighbor continued. "You know about his son, I suppose. The children's father."

Ash nodded. "Yeah."

There was a clap of wings overhead. Ash flinched and glanced up. A pigeon, launching from the chimney stack. And a face at the upstairs window, Callie's face. She pressed a finger to her lips and drew back into the gloom inside.

"Jumpy lad, aren't you?" said the woman.

"The pigeon," he said vaguely. "It startled me, that's all."

"Anyway," she said, "where was I?"

"Mr. Cullen's health."

"Ah yes." She sighed theatrically. "That terrible business with his son. I think that was the last straw. Broke his heart. Anyway, the children went off to stay with relatives in Thornditch, so I was told. I expect Mr. Cullen's house will be up for sale soon."

Thornditch. They didn't have any relatives there. They didn't have any relatives anywhere that Ash knew of, except for Grandpa Cullen. And now he knew that Callie was in the house anyway, hiding upstairs. Maybe she'd been secretly staying there all along.

"Thanks," said Ash. "Sorry for bothering you."

The woman smiled. "It's no bother, love. If you ask around Thornditch, I'm sure you'll find them soon enough. It's only a little village. Someone will know."

"Thanks," said Ash. "I will."

"What's your name, dear? So I can pass it on if I see anyone."

"Ash," he said. "Ash Tyler."

"Tyler? Robert Tyler's son?"

A hard edge in her voice now. She knew who his dad was. Ash should have kept his mouth shut.

"Don't you live in Thornditch?" she said.

"No," he said. Reddening at the lie. Forcing a smile, backing away. "Must be a different Tyler."

He walked off slowly, told himself it didn't matter. The woman didn't know much. Didn't know Mark was living wild in the mountains. Didn't even know that Callie was staying in Grandpa Cullen's house.

But she'd known he was lying, he was certain of it, and now perhaps she'd realize that Mark and Callie couldn't be in Thornditch. What if she started snooping?

And he still needed to talk to Callie.

Ash looked back. The neighbor was standing in the middle of the pavement, her arms folded, watching him go. He felt her gaze on him all the way to the end of the street.

Somehow he'd have to find another way to get to Callie.

IN THE END, IT WAS Callie who found Ash. As he headed toward the town center, she must have hurried along the back roads to catch up with him and suddenly there she was, walking out of an alley of broken stone and fireweed.

She walked beside him with her head bent, looking at the ground.

"Have you been living at your grandpa's house?" he said. "All this time? On your own?"

"I don't exactly live there. It's too risky. I go there to get food and change my clothes. Sometimes I spend the night there. I sneak in around the back after dark so the neighbors won't see me. I don't turn on the lights or make any noise and I keep away from the windows. Usually."

"That woman from next door thought you were staying with relatives in Thornditch."

"That's what Mark told her."

"Why?"

She shot him a strange look, half-annoyed and half-pitying. "Because we're alone. There isn't anyone to look after us, not now that Grandpa's in the hospital. They'd take us into child protective services if they knew."

"Right," he said. Face hot with embarrassment. "I might have blown your cover by accident. I think your neighbor knows that I'm from Thornditch and she's figured out that you can't be living there as well, otherwise I'd have known about it. I'm sorry."

Callie chewed her lip. "It's okay," she said at last. "At least now I know to steer clear. Just don't tell anyone that Mark and I are living on our own. Not even your mom. Promise me?"

"All right," Ash said, slowly. "I promise."

"Why did you come to the house anyway?"

"I was looking for you. I need to talk to you about Mark."

"What about him?" Callie asked.

Ash wasn't quite sure what to say. "I thought you might know more about what he's up to."

"He's still camping in the woods in the mountains, as far as I know."

"That's not what I mean."

"What, then?"

Ash bit his lip. He didn't want to tell her about his encounter with Mark and the hound boys, Mark wearing the dead stag's head and a cloak of dead birds. About Bone Jack. Not yet. Maybe never. "I don't know," he said. "He's acting really weird. I don't understand anything he says anymore."

Callie laughed. "And you think I do?"

They walked along in silence for a while, back on the main street now, voices and clatter and color and movement, the air stale with exhaust fumes.

"Where do you sleep when you don't go to your grandpa's house?" said Ash.

She shrugged. "Out in the mountains, here and there."

"Don't you have friends you could stay with?"

"Yeah. But if I stay with them, there'll be questions, and before you know it there'll be social workers involved and I could end up anywhere, miles away. So I avoid my friends. It's easier that way."

"What if they see you around? Like now, walking down the street?"

She gave a strange little smile. "When your mom's dead and your dad hanged himself and your brother's gone feral, your friends suddenly stop making much effort to be around you."

Ash fell silent, overwhelmed suddenly by the immensity of what she'd gone through, and by her loneliness. Then, softly, he said, "Aren't you afraid, all alone out in the mountains at night?"

"I've lived in the mountains my whole life. I'm not afraid of them."

"Maybe you should be," he said darkly. "There are things out there."

"What things?"

Your lunatic brother, he thought. Ghosts, maybe. Bone Jack . . . The words hung in his mind, unspoken.

"What things?" said Callie again.

Before he could answer, footsteps closed in behind them, then Ash felt a heavy arm across his shoulders. A freckled, sunburned face glossed with sweat pushing toward his. Grinning, breath that smelled of burger and ketchup. Chris Brooker. Liam Tunney a pace or two behind him.

Ash shoved Brooker away.

Brooker flung up his hands in mock surrender. "Whoa there, soldier boy! I'm just being friendly. I heard about your dad. Heard they had to send him home because he'd gone nuts." Still grinning, his eyes hard.

"What do you want?" said Ash. Backing away.

"Like I said, just wanted to see how you are. Soldier boy, stag boy. How's that carving on your chest? Healing up nicely?"

Ash took another step back, and another. He glanced across at Callie. She was staring at Chris Brooker as if she wanted to punch him.

"Earth and stone," hissed Brooker, "fire and ash, blood and bone."

Ash grabbed Callie's wrist. "Run," he said. "Come on!"

So they ran, dodging along the crowded pavement, between shoppers who swung wide-eyed faces at them like startled cattle.

Behind them, laughter, fast footfalls, angry passersby yelling.

"This way," said Callie. She pulled him with her across a courtyard, then into a crowded café and out through open glass doors to a terraced garden. An old man stared at them as they hurtled through, cup of tea stalled midway to his lips. Two women, a baby crying in a stroller. Ash twisted his body around the stroller, muttered, "Sorry, sorry."

Past a tortoiseshell cat curled up in the sunshine and out through a rickety green door into a narrow back alley that smelled of rotting cabbage. Ash followed Callie along a narrow passage between two garages to another alley and then another where they stopped to catch their breath, crouching among tall weeds beside a stone wall. The cuts on Ash's chest felt tight and hot and sore under the bandages. He looked down, half expecting to see blood seeping through his T-shirt, but there was nothing.

"That sweaty boy," said Callie. "What did he say? That stuff about earth and blood or whatever it was?"

"Earth and stone, fire and ash, blood and bone."

"What does that mean? Why did it make you run?"

"I don't know," said Ash. "I've heard it before, though. I heard Mark say it yesterday."

"What exactly went on that made you come and find me?"

"Mark . . ." He paused, wondering how much to tell her. "He left a note for me, telling me to meet him. I wasn't planning to go, but he found me out in the mountains and I followed him back to his camp in the woods. All the hound boys were waiting for me there. Mark must have set it up, I guess. Then he came out dressed as the stag god."

She shot him a sideways look. "Dressed as the what?"

Ash didn't answer right away.

"Tell me," she said. "I can't take any more secrets. My dad was like that before he killed himself. Now Mark. I've had enough of it. I know Mark has been into some strange stuff lately. Please. Just tell me."

Dark memories played through Ash's mind. Knife and blood, the severed stag's head, the stink of rotting meat. He didn't want to tell Callie about those things. They were too bleak, too horrifying.

But she had a right to know. And maybe she could help. So he started to talk and the words tumbled out, jumbled and urgent, a chaotic stream of consciousness. Ash told her all of it, not just the stuff about Mark but about Dad as well. She didn't stop him. She just crouched by the wall, listening, frowning.

Ash described the weird Stag Chase he'd seen up on the Leap and the shadows that raced along behind him afterward. He told her about Mark's threats to kill him if he ran as the stag boy, about the raggedy man in the mountains whom Mark had called Bone Jack and was determined to defeat. He told her about the wolf-dog, and about Mark as the stag god, and even about the stag's head that he'd carved into Ash's chest. He told her about Dad freaking out and about the black feather and the bloody handprint on the window and the sheep skull. How he thought Mark was trying to push Dad over the edge into madness, targeting Dad in order to scare Ash into pulling out of the Stag Chase.

He told her everything.

And then he waited.

CALLIE WAS QUIET FOR A long while, staring ahead at nothing. Ash's heart sank.

"Callie—"

"Shut up," she said. "I'm thinking. It's a lot to process."

So he shut up, tilted his head back and watched a gull cut silvery arcs against the pale sky. Nerves fluttered in his stomach.

"Grandpa and Dad used to tell us stories about Bone Jack and the Stag Chase," she said at last. "I always thought they were just folktales and ghost stories, a bit like fairy tales only rougher and scarier. But I've seen things too, out in the mountains."

"What sort of things?"

"I don't know. Like when you see movement out of the corner of your eye but when you look, there's nothing there. And sometimes . . ." She paused.

"Sometimes what?"

"Sometimes I see a man walking in the distance and then I look again and it's not a man, it's birds, crows, lots of them, flapping up."

Suddenly Ash's mouth felt dry. "What if it's both?" he

said. "A man made of birds, or a man who turns into birds? What if it's Bone Jack?"

"Maybe. I don't know." She shook her head in disbelief. "Those hound boys you said you saw in the woods with Mark— were they boys from school?"

"The ones in the woods yesterday were just local boys, I'm pretty sure of it, although I didn't know most of them. But the ones I saw that day on Stag's Leap—the day I saw you—were different. Almost solid but not quite, like mirages or something."

She nodded, solemn. "I saw them too."

"You told me you didn't!"

Callie shrugged. "I lied. I was angry with you."

"And now you're not?"

"A little. Not as much."

"Did you see where they went after they ran past me?"

"No. They vanished, like you said. They just sort of dissolved. Like mist does when the sun gets hot. Like they were . . ."

"Ghosts." Such a little word, a word that sounded almost like a whisper, but somehow saying it out loud and seriously to another person changed everything.

"Maybe."

"I don't even believe in ghosts," said Ash. "Not really. I keep thinking there must be a rational explanation for everything, even if I don't know what it is. Like the bird that flew into me. That could happen, right? A bird could accidentally fly into someone."

"I suppose so."

"But it happened to my dad too, twenty years ago, when he was the stag boy. During the Chase, a black bird—a crow or something—flew into him. And he saw something up on the Leap then too. Shadowy figures, he said, only they were shadows in color. They got into his head somehow, made him want to jump from the Leap. He almost did, but your dad saved him. Did you know that?"

"No," she said softly. "I had no idea."

"Then there's the Stag Chase we saw," said Ash. "And the lightning-fast wild man. No one moves that fast. It's not possible."

"Like you said, there has to be some kind of explanation, right?" Callie asked.

"Your brother said something about Bone Jack so I looked him up online. According to legend, Bone Jack is a mythic figure, from ancient times, with the ability to take different forms, so how can he possibly be real and living in the mountains right now? It doesn't make any sense. But it sounds like you've seen him too, and I can't explain all of it away, no matter how hard I try. Things have been happening that aren't supposed to happen in the real world but they keep happening right in front of me anyway. And Mark's in the middle of everything somehow. It always comes back to Mark or the Stag Chase or Bone Jack."

"What did Mark say about it all?"

Ash shrugged. "Only what I already told you. He's mad at me. That's fine. I let him down and he's still angry. I get that. But one minute he'll be like the old Mark again, like he's still my best friend. Then the next he'll come out with all this crazy stuff, about Bone Jack and the old ways and sacrifices to the land, telling me not to run in the Stag Chase because this year the stag boy is going to be killed. Killed by *him*. So I think some of what he's done, freaking out my dad and then the stag-god stuff in the woods, all that's just to scare me so I won't run."

"Do you think he means it? About killing the stag boy?"

"I don't know. He's so crazy right now that anything is possible."

Callie fell silent again.

"I'm sorry," said Ash. "If I'd been a better friend to him, maybe none of this would have happened."

"Maybe you should do what he says and pull out of the Stag Chase."

"I've thought about it. But I can't."

"Can't, or won't?"

He smiled. "Is there a difference?"

"Yeah, there is."

"If I don't run, I'll be running away from trouble again, like I did when your dad died and when I ran out on Mark. If I'd stuck around, maybe things wouldn't have gotten so bad. Maybe he wouldn't have gone so crazy."

"This might not be the best time to start feeling guilty."

"Maybe it is. Maybe it's exactly the best time."

"I think Mark's suffering from PTSD, like your dad," said Callie. "Only Mark got it after he found our dad hanging in the barn."

"It was Mark who found him?"

"Yes."

"He never told me that."

"He doesn't talk about it. I only know because I was there and he came running into the house, yelling that I had to call 911. I wanted to go into the barn, see for myself, but he wouldn't let me. He kept hold of me and wouldn't let me go. He protected me."

"I didn't know any of that."

Ash waited for Callie to get angry again, to tell him it was his own fault he didn't know because he'd run out on Mark. But instead she stood up and said, "Come on."

"Where to?"

"The library," she said. Then, sarcastically: "Have you ever been to a library?"

He gave her a withering look. "Yes. But not for a long time."

"Maybe we can find out more there," she said.

Ash nodded slowly. It was worth a try, he thought. He was tired of things not making sense, tired of always playing catch-up and of having no one to turn to, no one he could talk to about Mark and the spectral hound boys and Bone Jack. And Callie must feel the same way, maybe even more than he did because at least he had Mom and Dad. Callie had no one.

"Yeah," he said. "Good idea. I don't know how it all fits together but there must be some connection with the Stag Chase. If we can find out more about it, maybe we can figure out what's going on."

Ash smiled and Callie frowned back at him. "Why are you smiling?"

He shrugged. "I don't know. Because I told you every-thing and you believed me, right away, no questions."

"Sometimes you act like a coward," she said. "But I don't think you're a liar."

Ash stood up. "Come on, let's go."

They went through the back streets, in case Brooker and Tunney were still prowling the main street.

"I remember you and Mark always used to mess around on your bikes," said Callie. "Bombing downhill and getting banged up mostly. I didn't realize you were into running too. Now it seems like it's all you do."

Ash laughed. "Yeah, running is pretty much all I do lately."

"It's important to you, isn't it? The Stag Chase."

"Yeah, it is. My dad was the stag boy once. Now it's me."

"Keeping the tradition going, then."

"I guess, but it's more than that." He hesitated. "When I'm running, it's like . . . like I'm at the center of everything, holding it all together. And as long as I keep running, I can hold Dad together too. I don't know how. It's just a feeling. That if I run in the Stag Chase and I win, then maybe Dad will be all right." He laughed. "Sounds crazy, doesn't it?"

"A little. But maybe it's not."

They stopped. Looked up. "We're here."

COLDBROOK PUBLIC LIBRARY: A BIG, square building made of pale stone. Ash gazed up at it as he and Callie walked toward the door. He hoped they'd find some answers here, bits and pieces in dusty, long-forgotten books, obscure local histories, old documents—information that was nowhere to be found on the Internet.

Inside, the library was cool, airy and quiet. The librarian, a dark-haired man in his thirties, smiled at them as they walked past the checkout desk. There was a woman browsing the gardening section, another flipping through a book with a creepy clown's face on the cover, an old man reading a newspaper at a table. Ash and Callie wandered past shelves of crime novels, romance, science fiction, horror.

"Where should we start looking?" said Ash.

"The local-history section, I guess," said Callie.

"Where's that?"

Callie looked around helplessly. "I don't know. I'll ask."

She went off, came back with the dark-haired man.

"He's going to show us where to start," she said.

He led them through a labyrinth of shelving units and

partitions into a large sunlit room. "Anything in particular that you're looking for?"

"A history of the Stag Chase," said Callie.

"We've got one or two, I think," the librarian said. "And quite a few books on local folklore and traditions that will probably have a chapter or two about it."

"Thanks," said Ash.

The librarian smiled at him. "Folklore is a special interest of mine. Is this for a school project?"

"No," said Callie. She glanced at Ash. "He's the stag boy this year. We just wanted to know more about all the history and traditions of the Stag Chase."

Ash reddened.

"So you're the stag boy!" said the librarian. "I love the Stag Chase. I go every year to watch. You must have been training hard."

"Yeah," said Ash.

"Well, good luck with it. You'll find a few useful books in the section over by the window. I'll leave you to it. Let me know if you need any more help."

"We will," said Callie. "Thanks."

The section wasn't very big, just a couple of shelves with books on everything from haunted houses to a history of the Coldbrook folk dancers. They pulled out the books with the most promising titles. Eight books, all slim, dog-eared, old.

Ash eyed them. "We don't have to read them all, do we?"

"No. Just skim through and read any sections that look useful."

They sat down at a table. Ash picked up a book and started leafing through it. Ghost stories, strange bits of history, witches turned to stone, legends of giants who lived in caves in the mountains and kicked around boulders as if they were soccer balls. Nothing very useful. He put it down and the title of another book caught his eyes.

"This looks promising," he said. "*A History of the Thornditch Stag Chase* by Sybil Ingham. There has to be something in here."

It was more like a pamphlet than a book—thin, with a battered green cloth cover, published in 1910. Ash opened it up and began to read. "Looks like it's mostly about the Stag Chase in the nineteenth century," he said, disappointed. "There's just a short section at the front about the origins and early history."

"Better than nothing," said Callie. "What does it say?"

He read out loud to her.

The earliest known record of the Stag Chase is a reference to boys running in "Thornditch's Wyld Hunt" in a thirteenth-century poem. However, some archaeologists suggest that the stag's head carved on a standing stone near Corbie Tor locates the race's origins in the Dark Ages or earlier. According to oral tradition, the Stag Chase was once a form of human sacrifice in which the stag boy, if caught, was killed by the hounds as a blood offering to the gods. If true, this practice was abandoned or outlawed during the Middle Ages, though local lore has it that occasional blood sacrifices were still made for some centuries after.

"The human-sacrifice stuff is more or less what Mark told me that night you took me to see him in the woods," Ash said. "But I've never heard anything about a standing stone with the stag's head carved on it. Have you? The book says it's near Corbie Tor. I haven't heard of that either."

"I think it may be somewhere northwest, but I'm not sure," she said. "I bet Mark would know."

Ash turned more pages, skimming. Most of the book consisted of dull lists of the names of stag boys and notable hounds. But there were pictures too, pen-and-ink drawings of mountain scenes, a twisted hawthorn tree, a hare poised at the edge of a field.

Then his breath caught in his throat.

Bone Jack.

The floppy wide-brimmed hat, the eyes at once intense and faraway. The gaunt face.

There was no mistaking him.

"That's him," said Ash. "That's the man I met in the mountains. The man who was at Mark's camp."

"Are you sure?"

"Positive."

"I don't get it. That looks like a really old book," Callie said.

"It is. It says here that it was published in 1910."

"That's over a hundred years ago."

"I know. Look, I know this doesn't make any sense but I'm telling you I saw a figure yesterday, in the woods, and he looked *exactly* like this picture."

Callie drew a long breath. "This is all so crazy," she said.

"I've seen him three times now. Twice hanging around

the woods where Mark's camp is and once when I found the wolf I told you about. This picture is definitely him. Bone Jack."

"What does it say?"

"Not much. Just that the picture is of a wild man who lived in the mountains." He looked up from the book. "I looked up Bone Jack online too. There wasn't much about him, just a page in an online encyclopedia that said he was one of several mythic figures, wild men who lived in forests with birds and beasts. Every time I've seen him there have been crows around, or that wolf."

"Are you sure it was a wolf? Not one of those dog breeds that look like wolves?"

"I don't know. Bone Jack said it was a wolf but I've never seen one in the flesh and it was in such bad shape anyway, starving and plastered with dried mud. It could have been either, I guess."

"But where could it have come from? There aren't any wild wolves in Britain anymore."

"I know. I asked him about that too."

"What did he say?"

"He seemed to think it shouldn't have been there at all, that it got 'through,' almost as if it was from another century or another world or something."

"Okay," said Callie. "So let's say there really was a wolf in the mountains, even though British wild wolves died out hundreds of years ago. And there are ghost hound boys out there too. And there's Bone Jack, who you saw yesterday looking exactly the same as he does in a picture in a book published over a hundred years ago. The wolf and the ghosts and Bone Jack are all ancient, aren't they? They shouldn't be here. They should be dead and gone. So why are they here? What do they want? Why now?"

"I don't know. But it's not just now. I told you, my dad saw things twenty years ago when he was the stag boy."

"But the ghosts, or whatever they are, don't appear around the Stag Chase every year, do they? Sometimes people tell stories about seeing ghosts up on the mountains, like the stories my dad and grandpa used to tell me and Mark. But this isn't just a story. This is real. So why now?"

"Maybe it has something to do with Mark," Ash said. "Maybe he's summoned them."

"I don't think so. He's crazy and he's into all that ghosts and legends stuff but he doesn't have magic powers. He's just my brother."

"But maybe it's not about powers. Maybe it's about the land and its history. Mark said something about the land being sick with foot-and-mouth and drought, no sheep in the mountains anymore, everything withering and dying. He said that's why the old ways are coming back. The sicker the land is, the stronger its ghosts get."

Callie sighed. "So what do we do now?"

"That's it for today, I guess. I'd better get back home before Mom starts worrying. Tomorrow I'm going to find Mark."

She shook her head. "He won't talk to you. I'll go. I'll find him."

"Why? I'm caught up in all of this too. Some of it's partly

my fault. I want to know what's going on. I need to try to make things right."

"I know, but he's still angry with you. He might talk to me about it, but he won't do it if you're there."

Ash scowled but deep down he knew she was right. Mark would put on an act if he was there, make threats, swagger around like he did the night Callie had taken Ash to his camp. "Okay," he said at last. "But promise me you'll tell me exactly what he says."

"I will. I promise."

They put the books back on the shelves and stopped to thank the librarian on their way out. "Did you find what you wanted?" he said.

Ash nodded. "Yeah, we found a few things."

"Good. I expect I'll see you on Sunday at the Stag Chase, then. I hope you have a good race, leave the hounds in the dust."

"Thanks," said Ash. "I'll do my best."

They left the library, walked back to the main street, thronged with people.

Callie stopped. "I guess I'll head home now too. Mark could be anywhere and it's getting late. I'll go out looking for him in the morning."

"Where will you stay tonight? You could come back to my house, only—"

"Yeah, your dad. I know. I couldn't stay with you anyway. There'd be too many questions."

"Where, then?"

"I haven't decided yet. Not back to Grandpa's house. It's too risky now. Maybe back to the farm."

"The farm? The farm's all boarded up," he said. "Isn't it?"

She looked away, wouldn't meet his gaze. "There's a way in around the back," she said. "It's all right, seriously. It was our home."

"Yeah, I know, but . . ." Ash felt cold and sick inside at the thought of Callie spending nights there, alone in that silent house in the vast mountain darkness, only yards away from where her dad had hanged himself. "It's creepy."

"I know," she said. "But everything's so weird anyway that it doesn't matter."

"Callie . . . ," he said. He was about to say that he'd come with her, stay with her so she wouldn't be alone, but she was already backing away from him. Another step, then another, then she turned and was lost in the throng of shoppers.

Ash stood for a few long moments watching the crowd where she'd disappeared. Then, alone, too weary now to walk or run home, he headed back to the bus stop.

MIDNIGHT. TWO MORE DAYS UNTIL the Stag Chase. Ash tossed and
turned in his bed, half-awake, half-dreaming. He dreamed
the spectral stag boy was in his bedroom. Clay-daubed skin
like cracked stone, charcoal making hollows of his eyes, the
dark gash of his mouth. "Earth and stone," the stag boy
said. Singsong, his voice soft as a breeze, as cold as death's
breath. "Fire and ash, blood and bone."

Behind the stag boy, shadows gathered. They loomed
above him, folded over him like a black wave. A tide of piti-
less dark. The boy sank away into it as if he was drowning.

"Wait for me!" Ash tried to say. But his mouth wouldn't
open. The words jammed in his throat. He flung off the bedsheet and stumbled across the room to where the stag boy
had been. Followed him into the deep darkness. Then he
was pushing through leaf and twig. Underfoot there wasn't
carpet anymore; instead he walked barefoot on the dry leaf
litter of a woodland floor.

No sign of the stag boy. Nothing except the dark shapes
of trees, a star-scattered sky, moonlight.

He emerged from among the trees onto a stretch of
scrubby, stony land. He stopped and stared. He'd been here

before. The shallow, shrunken stream. The thorn trees.
Bone Jack's stone hut.

The windows were dark.

He went closer.

A chill wind rattled the bone strings in the doorway.
Beyond them, someone or something moved in the gloom.

The face at the window. Pale, blurred.

The quick beat of Ash's own heart, the ocean sound of
rushing blood in his ears.

He went closer.

No one there.

A movement nearby. Wing beats, then soft footsteps.

Suddenly Bone Jack was standing in front of him. "You
shouldn't be here, lad. Go home."

Then all of it was gone, blacked out in a blink.

Ash was still in his bedroom, standing, facing the wall.

The cry of an owl in the trees.

He went to the window, looked out.

Below on the lawn stood a silent pack of masked hound
boys. Their heads were tilted upward. From behind their
masks, they watched him.

Ash stepped back. He crouched down, below the level
of the windowsill, then he crept forward again, peered out
around the edge of the curtain.

The hound boys were gone. There was just moonlit
grass, the black trees beyond it. Nothing to suggest they'd
ever even been there.

Shivering, he got back into bed. He thought about
Callie, out there alone in the night. He thought about Mark,

clay-painted, wearing the stag's head, cloaked in bloodied crow skins. He thought about Dad.

Fear burned through Ash like a fever. The bedsheets stuck to his sweat-slick skin.

Night crowded in, hot and heavy, pressing down on him. He hardly knew if his eyes were open or closed. The darkness around his bed filled with footsteps, whispers, a rain of leaves falling slowly and silently. Ghosts calling to him and he had to follow, he had to, but he couldn't move.

"Come with us," they said. "Come with us." Ash's body was deadweight, his chest so tight he could barely draw breath. With a huge effort, he sat up.

Nothing under him except empty darkness, and he was falling. He clawed at empty air, his throat filled with screams.

He hit the rocks hard. Felt his flesh bruise and tear, his bones shatter, the hot rain of his own blood. A hiss of air escaped his lips.

He heard Bone Jack's voice again. "Go home," it said, full of menace. "Stay away."

His eyes snapped open.

Daylight. Ash was lying on his back in bed, arms flung out wide, the sheet twisted around his legs.

A knock at the door, then it opened and Mom came in. "Ash?" she said. "Are you all right?"

He fumbled with the bedsheet, pulling it up to his chin so she wouldn't see the bandages covering the cuts on his chest.

"Yeah, I'm fine," he said.

His voice was thin and scratchy. His skin still so hot.

"You were yelling," said Mom. "And I thought I heard someone else's voice in here with you."

Ash glanced around the room. Just in case. "There's no one here," he said. "It must have been the radio."

"Well, I definitely heard you yell out. Did you have a nightmare?"

"Uh, yeah, I guess I must have."

"Do you want to talk about it?"

He shrugged. "I can't really remember it. I dreamed I was falling."

"I get those dreams too sometimes." She crossed the room and opened the curtains wide. Sunlight poured in. "Lots of people do. It has something to do with going to sleep too quickly and your mind getting out of sync with your body. It feels like you're falling, then you jerk awake again."

She sat on the edge of Ash's bed and pressed her cool hand to his forehead. "You've got a bit of a temperature," she said.

"I'm okay. It's just hot in here."

"You've had a lot to deal with lately, what with all your training and Dad coming home and then seeing Mark again."

"Yeah," said Ash. "I guess so."

"You should take it easy now until the race. You need plenty of sleep and good food. Mom's orders. No more of these punishing training runs. You're supposed to wind down your training before a big race anyway, so a couple days of rest won't hurt."

He looked at her. Her angular, almost beautiful face. The delicate shadows under her eyes. She looked tired and sad.

"Mom," he said. "The other night. Dad went out, really late. I followed him."

Worry creased her forehead. "When was this?"

"The night before he took me out fishing and had a meltdown on Tolley Carn."

"Why didn't you tell me this sooner?"

"I don't know. I guess because you were already so worried."

"You don't need to protect me, Ash. In fact, I'd rather you didn't try. It's my job to protect *you*. I need to know what's going on, no matter what it is."

Ash nodded.

"So where did he go? What happened?" she asked.

"He went to Stag's Leap first, then the Cullen farm. He stood there, at the gate, staring at the house. Then he saw me. I think he knew I was there all along actually but he didn't let on. We walked home together. He seemed all right, a bit down, that's all."

Mom gave a small, sad smile. "It's not so strange," she said. "Not if you think about it. Tom and him, they went back a long way. They were close friends when they were boys. Like you and Mark."

"Yeah, that's what Dad said."

"I think he misses Tom more than he lets on. Did he tell you that Tom saved his life once?"

"Yes. He said something happened on the Leap when he was the stag boy, and Tom pulled him back from the edge."

Mom nodded. "It won't always be like this, you know," she said. "Things will get better, I promise."

"Yeah," he said, turning away from her. "But when?"

She stood up, went to the door. "I still think you've got a little fever," she said. "Try to get some more sleep, just rest for today. No more running until the Stag Chase. Promise me?"

"Okay," Ash said. Closing his eyes, already drifting toward sleep again, Mom's voice mingling with half-formed dreams.

22

HE HEARD THE DOOR CLICK shut as Mom went out. Heat wrapped around him like a warm wet blanket. Even with the curtains drawn, with his eyes closed, there was an aching brightness. He tossed and turned and couldn't get comfortable.

A tinny crackle of music from the radio downstairs. A dog barking in the distance.

A crow flying straight at the window, beak the color of iron, claws hooked out.

Ash bolted upright.

He looked out the window. Nothing but pale sky.

Perhaps he had dreamed the crow. Or he was seeing things, losing his mind little by little. He shivered. Nothing seemed certain or solid or stable anymore. Sometimes he felt like he couldn't even trust his own senses, his own thoughts.

He got dressed, carefully rolling his T-shirt down over his bandaged chest. Then he went downstairs to the kitchen. The house was quiet and felt empty, though he knew Dad was almost certainly upstairs, shut in his darkened room as usual.

Sometimes it felt as if his dad was slowly ceasing to exist, his presence fading a little more every day.

Ash glanced at the wall clock. Two o'clock in the afternoon already. He must have slept again for longer than he'd thought.

By now, Callie had probably found Mark, talked to him. Ash thought about going to Mark's camp again to look for them, but he knew instinctively that it was a bad idea. Callie had told him to keep away and she'd be furious if he barged in. When she was ready, she'd tell him all about it. He just had to trust her and wait.

He remembered the book they'd found in the library, the reference to a standing stone with a stag's head carved into it, and to somewhere called Corbie Tor. Landscape features he'd never heard of before.

He made himself a sandwich and went back up to his bedroom, eating as he searched online for Corbie Tor. It didn't take long to find it, in an article on an antiquarian maps website. An "obsolete archaic place name," the article said. At least that explained why he'd never heard of it. Ash clicked on a link and an image of an old map opened up. It was clumsily drawn, a crude sketch of the mountainous region northwest of Thornditch. But it was accurate enough for him to figure out where Corbie Tor must be.

He could go there this afternoon, look around, see if he could find the standing stone. And there was a chance he'd see Bone Jack again out there too. The thought made him edgy but he didn't care anymore. The Stag Chase was the day after tomorrow and he wanted to find out whatever he could before he ran.

He pulled on his sneakers. He'd promised Mom he wouldn't run today, but walking would take too long, so he grabbed his bike, a mean-looking hardtail he'd bought two summers ago after saving up for a whole year. He took the side roads and the main walking trails, then went along the old drovers' paths.

He stopped.

Ash recognized this spot. The gnarly thorn tree next to the lichen-mapped boulder. Corbie Tor must be the old name for that great knuckle of rock jutting from the mountainside ahead.

This was where he'd found the wolf, he was sure of it.

In the valley below he saw the stream and more thorn trees, and beyond those, the rocky ground where Bone Jack's stone hut was.

Ash left his bike at the side of the path and climbed up onto the higher ground above it.

Ahead stood a lone figure, silhouetted against the sky.

Callie.

She started heading north and he followed. The air was so still that every sound he made seemed huge. The crackle of the dry heather underfoot, the rasp of his breath.

He watched as Callie reached Corbie Tor and vanished around the other side of it.

Ash crept closer.

Suddenly he heard voices. Callie's of course, and then Mark's. Ash stopped and listened but he couldn't make out their words.

Ash watched them walk out from the shadow of Corbie Tor and onto the lower path. Mark stood half-naked, clay-daubed, his hair sticking up in stiff spikes. He looked like some wild warrior from the ancient past, and suddenly, Callie, with the mountain breeze tugging at her hair, seemed no less wild than her brother.

There was a closeness about them Ash had never really noticed before. He saw it now, in the way they moved with the same loose, easy strides, and the way word and gesture shifted between them, subtle and somehow secretive.

Suddenly Ash felt like an intruder. Callie had told him to stay away, to let her talk to Mark alone. He should have listened.

He turned to leave, started walking back toward where he'd left his bike. Then he stopped, annoyed. He was part of this madness too, caught up in everything just like Mark and Callie were. He had every right to be there with them. There were things he needed to know, questions he couldn't let go.

"Hey!" Ash called out to them.

Mark glanced back and the spell broke.

He and Callie waited for Ash to catch up, watched him blunder toward them through the bracken.

Callie glared at him. "I told you not to come."

"Yeah, well, I have just as much a right to be here as you. Besides, I wasn't looking for you or Mark," said Ash. "I thought you'd be at his camp in the woods, not out here."

"So why did you come here, then?"

"I'm looking for the places we read about in that book."

She scowled at him. "Well, you might as well stay, now that you're here."

They walked on in silence, following Mark.

The sun shone bright in Ash's eyes. Gnats danced about him. He swatted them away and tried to catch Callie's attention again but she avoided looking at him. He understood. She was here for Mark, not for him.

Mark stopped.

A thread of skylark song spiraled down from above.

"What now?" said Ash.

Mark pointed toward a spike of rock Ash had never seen before, jutting from a bed of heather. It was maybe eight feet tall, solitary, bleak. The stone mentioned in the book he and Callie had looked at in the library. It had to be.

"Is that what you came to find?" said Mark.

Ash nodded. "The standing stone, yeah."

They went up to it.

At first all Ash could see was pitted, weatherworn stone, scabbed with lichen. Then he ran his fingertips over the sun-warmed surface. From the rough contours a shape started to emerge.

Antlers. A stag's head. And not just a head. He could make out a torso and limbs as well. A figure that was half-human, half-stag. It looked wild and powerful.

Mark laughed. "Do you know what it is?"

"Of course I know what it is," said Ash. "It's a stag boy."

"Why do you think it's here, on this stone?"

"I don't know. Maybe it's some sort of ancient marker, some pagan thing to do with the Stag Chase."

"It's where they used to sacrifice the stag boys, in the early days," Mark said. "They'd drag them here, cut their throats and watch as their blood ran down the stone into the earth. Later on, when the holy men came and preached against human sacrifice, they stopped bringing the stag boys here. They chased them off the Leap instead, or threw them off. Far from the priests' prying eyes. That's where Stag's Leap gets its name from—the stag boy's leap."

"How do you know all that?"

"I just know," said Mark. "Stories my grandpa used to tell us. Old books."

"Even if some of those stories are true," said Ash, "all that stuff was thousands of years ago. It's ancient history."

He looked at Callie. She didn't look angry anymore, only tired, defeated somehow, her face drawn and her eyes bright with tears.

"The old days are gone," continued Ash. "No one is sacrificed these days. It's just a race now."

"Not this year it's not. You know. You've seen things." Mark paused. "You know."

"I don't know what I've seen. Everything seems so messed up. All I know is that a few things have happened that I can't explain and there are a lot of old legends and ghost stories about dark stuff from the past."

"It isn't just stuff from the past," said Mark. "That's why you've got to pull out of the Stag Chase. Now, while there's still time. I'm serious, Ash. Pretend you've torn a muscle or twisted your ankle. They can find another stag boy."

Ash blinked the sunlight from his eyes. He'd had enough. "Why are you doing all this, Mark?" He was almost shouting. "What do you want?"

"I told you. Look around. There's nothing here. The

sheep are all dead. Thousands of years of people keeping sheep on this land, and they're all gone. Everything completely parched, and the streams drying up. The land is dying. And it's not just here. The whole world is dying only most of the time we pretend it isn't, we pretend it's all okay. That's what killed my dad, knowing that. He lost everything, lost our mom and then the sheep and then the land. And then he gave up, he couldn't fight anymore. But I haven't given up. I'm still fighting. And I've found a way to make things right, to bring back my dad and to heal the land."

Ash glanced at Callie. "What about Callie? What about what she wants?"

"I know what's best for my own sister."

Callie lifted her head. Her face was drawn, her gray eyes dark and fierce. "Mark, this is crazy," she said. "There are other ways we can help heal the land. No one needs to be killed. Nothing's going to bring Dad back. He's gone. This is it, this is all we've got. The three of us, and Grandpa. And Grandpa's sick. We should be with him, we should be helping him. Not standing around out here in the middle of nowhere, talking about killing stag boys."

"Callie—" Mark took a step toward her but she backed away.

"I can't listen to you anymore," she said. "I can't listen to all this talk about Dad, about killing people. Stop it. You have to stop."

She continued backing away.

"Callie," said Ash, "it's all right. Please don't—"

But she wouldn't even look at him. Instead she turned and ran off up the path.

Ash started to follow her but Mark stopped him. "Let her go. She doesn't get it."

"Doesn't get what?" said Ash. "That you think if you paint yourself with clay and kill crows and murder the stag boy it's going to bring your dad back? Maybe there are ghosts out there but no one comes back from the dead. Not really. Even if you kill me or some other stag boy, it won't solve everything. It won't save the land and it won't bring back your dad."

"You're wrong," said Mark. His voice was quiet and deadly serious. "You can bring people back. There's a way. Blood for blood, life for life." He glanced toward Bone Jack's stone hut in the valley below. "Him," he said. "Bone Jack. The guardian of the boundary between life and death. The stories say if you can get past him, you can get past death itself."

"So what then?" said Ash. "You're going to sacrifice the stag boy and Bone Jack's going to let you bring your father back from the dead? That's insane."

Mark's eyes glittered. "You still don't understand who Bone Jack is, what he is."

Ash wanted Mark to shut up. He wanted things to make sense again. "Bone Jack's just a weird man, a hermit who lives in the mountains," he said, even though he didn't believe it himself.

"He's a shaman," said Mark. "He moves between the land of the living and the land of the dead. He's thousands of years old and he shapeshifts. One minute he's a man, the next he's a bird. Then a hundred birds. You know it as well as I do. And when he shapeshifts, when he breaks apart into crows, that's when I can get at him. I've been killing his crows, a few here, a few there. Every time I do it, he gets weaker. When I take the crows and make them mine, I take his strength. And when I've taken enough of it, I'll be able to do what he can do. I'll go into Annwn, into the realm of the dead, and I'll bring back my dad."

"So that's why you're really out here? Waiting for Bone Jack to shapeshift so you can kill some more crows, take Bone Jack's power and travel to the land of the dead? Is that the plan?"

"It's part of it."

"Mark," said Ash, "you're sick. You should come home with me. Please come home with me."

"I'm not sick," said Mark. "And I'm not going anywhere."

Ash looked away from him, looked beyond the standing stone. There was something else out there, a hundred yards or so farther along the path, a familiar shape silhouetted against the sky.

He went toward it.

The stag's head, the one Mark had worn as a headdress when he'd dressed up as the stag god. Stuck on a pole. Its eyes gone, eaten away. Its coat dull, matted with dried blood. Flies droning around it.

Ash turned away from it and walked back toward Mark. Mark smiled weirdly, eyes flint-hard. Ash watched him smirk and swagger.

"I'm going to run in the Stag Chase," said Ash. "I'm going to run for my dad. I'm going to run all your ghosts into the ground. You can't stop me."

He kept walking, left Mark behind. He climbed up Corbie Tor. He looked down across the valley to where Bone Jack's stone hut stood among the thorn trees.

On the ridge beyond, dark birds gathered like a storm cloud. They flowed and eddied in the warm air, flapped apart, drew together again, closer now, denser, wings touching, melting into one another until the flock became a shadow, an outline. The silhouette of a man in a long coat, a wide-brimmed hat.

Ash glanced down to where Mark had been standing but Mark was nowhere to be seen.

Ash was alone except for Bone Jack—the wild man, the shapeshifter, dark against the skyline. And Ash watched him stride away until he couldn't see him anymore.

Ash waited a few minutes longer, until he was sure Bone Jack wasn't coming back soon, then he set off down the mountainside.

23

ASH DIDN'T HAVE A PLAN, didn't know what to do exactly, what he was looking for. Something, anything, that might give him an edge on Mark.

He stopped outside Bone Jack's hut.

The bone strings in the doorway rattled in the breeze. Beyond them was deep shadow. The same as last time, except now the filthy windows were blank and there was no blurry face staring through at him.

He listened. All he heard was the slow slide of his own breathing, the whisper of the breeze among the thorn trees, bird chatter.

No sign of Bone Jack. Not that that meant anything. If Bone Jack really was all that Ash was starting to believe he was, he could arrive in the blink of an eye.

Ash drew a deep breath and pushed through the bone strings into hot dusty gloom. Sweat prickled on his skin. He stopped a little way inside, waited for his eyes to adjust to the dark. Taut threads of sunlight cut through the grime on the windows. The tiny skulls on the bone strings threw weird shadows against the back wall.

Now he could make out shapes in the gloom. A small table with two chairs. A woodstove with a stack of firewood next to it. A pile of blankets and furs at one end of the room.

It seemed more like a den than a home.

Something moved, fluttered and flapped. He froze, heart thudding. But it was only a tiny bird, a wren maybe. It shot past him, out through the bone curtain.

Ash went farther inside. A fox skull on a shelf, an old army knife, five stones set out side by side on the table. He picked one up, felt its weight and balance. Leaf-shaped, shiny, cool against his skin. A flint arrowhead.

Next to the arrowheads was a book. It was small, bound with old soft leather. He opened it. The thin pages were so fragile that he imagined even the gentlest touch of his fingertips might tear them. There was writing on them, a poem, handwritten in inky lettering.

"You again, lad," said a voice behind him.

Ash spun around, still clutching the book. Fear shook through him.

Bone Jack stood in the doorway, silhouetted against the bright sunlight outside. "What is it this time? Another sick wolf? Thieving? Snooping?"

Ash shot a panicky glance across at the nearest window, briefly wondered whether it would break if he hurled himself against it.

"I saw you over yonder with the girl and the painted boy," said Bone Jack. "The crazy boy who's been killing my crows."

"He's killing them to take your power. You could stop him. You *should* stop him."

"I can't stop him. Things has to play out as they will." His eyes were sharp and cold as ice.

"Are the legends true? The ones that say you're a shapeshifter?" said Ash. The words rushing out, taking him by surprise. "Or something else? A spirit or a mythical being, like Taliesin or the Green Man?"

"They're just names," said Bone Jack. "Names and stories. Some of them's true, some of them's not."

Fear twisted inside Ash. He felt trapped, Bone Jack standing between him and the doorway. He took a deep breath to steady his nerves. "I came here to find some answers, that's all. I've seen strange things in the mountains. A stag boy running and hound boys chasing him. Then there was that wolf. And Mark's saying he's going to kill the stag boy and bring his dad back from the dead but somehow it all seems to have something to do with you."

As he spoke, Ash took a step toward the door. Legs heavy as wood, sweating so much his shirt was sticking to his back.

Bone Jack stayed where he was, blocking the only way out.

"It ain't about me," said Bone Jack. "It's about the dying land and the old ways."

"That's what Mark said. The old ways. Life for life. The stag boy's life in exchange for his dad's."

"The dead stay dead," said Bone Jack. "Only ghosts come back."

"Like those hound boys?"

150

Bone Jack nodded.

"Why have they come back?"

"They're here every year, every Stag Chase. Most years there's nothing much to them. But now the land's sick and its darkest dreams are rising from it like mist. The sicker the land is, the stronger they get."

"What do they want?"

"Blood and death is what. It's all they know. How to hunt, how to kill."

"Can't you stop them?"

No response. Bone Jack's face was hidden in the shadow under the brim of his hat and suddenly Ash couldn't catch his breath. The gloom pressed in around him, thick with ancient dust, and all he could think about was getting outside, into fresh air and sunlight and limitless space.

"I'll go now," Ash said. His voice was a croak. He took a small step toward the door, then another. "I'm sorry I disturbed you."

He kept his gaze low, kept moving, slow tiny paces.

Bone Jack stepped aside to let him out.

Ash kept walking until he was halfway across the clearing. Then he stopped, his fear fading in the sunlight. He looked back at Bone Jack.

"I don't know what to do," said Ash. "What should I do?"

"Hold to your own, lad."

"What does that mean?"

But Bone Jack had already turned away, retreated into the gloom behind the bone strings.

Ash ran on through the trees and up the slope back toward Corbie Tor. Halfway, he stopped.

He was still holding the book he'd picked up in the hut.

He sat on a slab of rock and stared at it. There was a faint trace of lettering on the cover, so faded that he could barely make out the words. He angled the book into the sunlight, squinted at it, spoke its title out loud: "*The Battle of the Trees.*"

He'd come across that title before. Where? He trawled his memory. Then he realized: He'd seen it when he'd looked up Bone Jack online and learned about his connection to those other mysterious wild men of the mountains. Taliesin, he thought. *The Battle of the Trees* was a poem written by Taliesin.

The breeze gusted, hot and dry.

He opened the book and started to read.

> I have been in a multitude of shapes,
> Before I assumed a consistent form.
> I have been a sword, narrow, variegated,
> I will believe when it is apparent.
> I have been a tear in the air,
> I have been the dullest of stars.
> I have been a word among letters,
> I have been a book in the origin.
> I have been the light of lanterns,
> A year and a half.

A poem about shapeshifting.

The breeze blew harder, lashed tears from Ash's eyes

and tore at the tissue-thin pages. He slammed the book shut and shielded it from the wind with his body. But it broke into pieces in his hands. Shreds of paper danced like flakes of ash across the mountainside. All that was left in his hands were a few limp scraps of old leather.

Gone. Only the echo of the poem in his mind.

I have been in a multitude of shapes . . .

Birdman. Shapeshifter.

Bone Jack.

The wind dropped. Ash stood up.

In his mind, he heard Bone Jack's voice again. *Hold to your own, lad.*

"What does that mean?" Ash repeated, out loud.

Perhaps Bone Jack had meant that he should make his own choices and stand by them. Or that he should take care of his own—of Mom and Dad—and leave the rest alone. But maybe Mark and Callie were his own too.

Or maybe Bone Jack had meant something else, that Ash's fate was already written, that there was nothing he could do to change it.

Every potential answer only seemed to lead to more questions. And maybe none of it mattered anyway. Maybe all that mattered was the one thing Ash knew he could do: run.

Only tomorrow to get through and then it would be Sunday, the day of the Stag Chase. Until then, he'd sleep, chill out, play computer games, load up on carbs, keep his head down. Then on Sunday he'd run. Everything was simple when he ran, just muscle and bone, rhythm and focus and the lay of the land. Nothing and no one would catch him. He'd outrun them all. Mark, the hound boys, the ghosts. He'd leave them all trailing in his wake. He'd run the race his own way, and Dad would be waiting for him at the finish line. It would be all right. He just had to run and everything would be all right.

A movement below in the valley caught his eye. Crows, flapping up from the thorn trees.

The air thrummed with their wing beats. They scattered across the land, night-black rags tossed on the wind, and Ash watched them until they were gone.

THAT NIGHT, ASH SLEPT DEEPLY, dreamlessly. When he awoke, the house was quiet. These days it was almost always quiet. Dad had been home nearly two weeks, and the silence and tension almost seemed ordinary now. Mom either in the garden or out somewhere. Dad curled up in the dark in his room. A new normal they'd all somehow fallen into, learned to live with.

Ash glanced at his alarm clock. Just past eight thirty. Saturday morning.

The Stag Chase was tomorrow.

Excitement and fear burned through him. He rolled out of bed, got dressed, went downstairs. He stopped on the landing and knocked softly on the door to Dad's room. No response, but he went in anyway.

He switched on the light and saw the bed was empty and unmade. Sheets trailing to the floor. The backpack sat slumped against the wall, still spilling clothes. The air was sour with sweat and dread.

Dad was next to the window, squatting on his heels with his back to the wall. He was twitchy. He kept sniffing as if he had a cold. Rubbed his hand over his face again and again. In the hard white light, he looked gray and ill.

"What are you doing down there? Dad? Are you okay?"

No reply.

Ash waded through all the junk to where Dad was. He pulled back the curtains and opened the window. Fresh air, sunlight, and a rush of birdsong.

"Shut the window!" snapped Dad. "Shut the curtains."

Ash stared at him. "Come on, Dad. Get up. Please get up, Dad."

"Shut the window," said Dad again. "Shut the curtains."

Silently Ash did as he was told. He switched off the light, closed the door behind him. He trembled and felt sick. As if the world had tilted and rearranged itself in ways he couldn't understand. Something gone wrong, gone askew, throwing everything off-kilter, and he didn't even know what it was, never mind how to fix it.

Ash went outside. He sat on the doorstep and stared at the sun until it burned away everything—land and sky and memory.

Then the door opened behind him. Mom came out, wearing her floppy hat, pruning shears in her hand.

"Scoot over," she said, and sat next to him. "Are you sitting here thinking about tomorrow's race?"

"Yeah, a little," he said. "And about Dad. I went into his room earlier. He was crouched down in the dark, by the window."

"I know," she said. "He's having a bad day."

"He's not going to make it to the Stag Chase tomorrow, is he?"

"We'll see. He might have a better day tomorrow." Her face softened and she gave a small smile. "What about you? Are you ready for the race?"

"Yeah, as ready as I'll ever be."

"You'll be great. I know you will."

Ash looked at his mom and felt a million miles away from her. She didn't know about Mark's threats or the spectral hound boys with murder in their eyes or Bone Jack. To her, the Stag Chase was just a race and all he had to worry about was running. And that was how it had to be. If he told her even half of it, she'd make him pull out of the race and he needed to run, needed to win, to make Dad proud, to give Dad something to hold on to.

So he nodded and said, "Yeah, I'll be fine."

"Any plans for today?" she said.

He laughed. "Big plans. I'm going to play computer games, eat a lot of carbs, lounge around and sleep as much as I can."

Mom smiled. "You'd better get started, then."

Hours later, Ash had done about as much relaxing as he could stand. He was sure he'd lie awake half the night worrying about the race, about Dad, about Mark. Instead he fell asleep almost immediately when his head hit the pillow.

Until something woke him. A sound. He lay in the moon-washed dark, his eyes wide open, his heart racing.

It came again—a thud, then a grunt of breath.

He got out of bed, opened the curtain and looked out.

He expected to see hound boys gathered outside again. But this time there was only one boy out there in the moonlight, bone-white under a ragged black cloak and with the monstrous stag's head upon his shoulders.

Ash knew it was Mark, in his stag-god guise, but still his heart quickened and a chill ran through him. A thin pain threaded along the cuts on his chest, as if the ghost of the knife was retracing its bloody path across his skin.

Mark didn't look up. He raised one foot and brought it down hard, then the other foot, again and again, slowly at first, building to a steady rhythm. He raised his arms and the cloak hung from them like half-opened wings. Then he danced, circling like a huge grotesque bird. He didn't look up. Whatever this was, it wasn't meant for Ash's eyes.

So what was it? Maybe a pre–Stag Chase ritual? Or maybe something else.

Ash pulled on a T-shirt and went downstairs.

By the time he got outside, Mark was gone.

He'd left the stag's head behind, though, propped upright in the middle of the moon-silvered lawn. It seemed to watch Ash from the inky hollows where its eyes had once been. Bone gleamed through its tattered hide. The stench of death hung in the still night air, rotten and sickly sweet.

He couldn't leave it here for Mom to find in the morning. But he couldn't shove it under the hedge like he'd done with the sheep skull. The antlers were too big, too unwieldy, and the hedge wouldn't hide the stink of it anyway.

Breathing through his mouth to avoid the smell, he grasped the antlers and lifted. It was heavy, strapped to a clumsy wooden structure that Mark must have added so he could position it on his shoulders, the stag's head raised above his own. Ash held it at arm's length and tried not to think about the putrefying flesh and the likelihood of maggots, or about Mark, so far gone in his madness that he could bear to wear the foul thing.

Ash carried it to the road, then swung it up over the hedge into the field opposite the house. It thumped down somewhere in the darkness beyond, among nettles and foxgloves.

He went back to the house, headed straight for the kitchen. He took a clean cloth from the cabinet under the sink, ran it under hot water and squirted soap all over it. He washed his hands, his arms, his legs, everywhere the stag's rotten head might have touched him or dripped putrid filth on him.

A door opened upstairs, the pad of footsteps on the landing, then coming down.

Quickly Ash dried himself with a tea towel, opened the fridge and pretended to root around inside it.

The kitchen door opened and he blinked owlishly at Mom.

"It's two o'clock in the morning," she said. "What are you doing in here?"

"I couldn't sleep," Ash said.

"So you thought you'd come downstairs and make yourself a snack?"

159

He grinned sheepishly. "I was hungry."

"You shouldn't eat this late at night, especially when you've got a race to run in a few hours. Come on, go back to bed."

He shut the fridge door, followed Mom upstairs. "Try to get some sleep," she said. "And if you can't sleep, at least get some rest."

Back in his bedroom, Ash glanced out the window again. The night was still, silent except for the fluting of a tawny owl. It was as if Mark had never been there.

Ash lay down on the bed and closed his eyes. He was too tired now to worry anymore about Mark or anything else. He knew the feeling wouldn't last but for now he let himself drift with it. Morning would come. The Stag Chase would go ahead. And there would be no turning back.

HE SLEPT UNTIL SEVEN, WOKE to a jabber of voices on his radio alarm. For a few minutes he didn't move, just lay with his eyes wide open, staring at the patterns of hazy sunlight playing across the ceiling. This was it. The day of the Stag Chase. Today anything could happen, the glory of victory or the disgrace of losing, life or death.

Glory. Please let it be glory. And life.

Ash jackknifed out of bed, pulled on his tracksuit and running shoes, went downstairs.

Mom was in the kitchen.

"Morning," he said. "Where's Dad?"

"He's not up yet, love," said Mom.

"But he knows, right? He knows it's the Stag Chase today?"

"Yes, he knows. He'll come down soon, I'm sure." But she didn't sound sure. "Sit down and I'll get you some breakfast," she said. "Come on."

Ash sat at the table. Mom put a bowl of oatmeal in front of him. Now he felt sick, nerves jumping like grasshoppers in his stomach. He forced himself to eat, gluey spoonful after gluey spoonful. Then a slice of toast spread with peanut butter and honey.

Quarter to eight and still no sign of Dad. Ash couldn't relax. "I'll go wake him up," he said.

He went upstairs, entered the dark room again. He wrinkled his nose at the sourness of the clogged air. Dad lay hunched on his side in bed. Even before he spoke, Ash knew Dad wasn't going to make it. Today was another of his bad days.

"Dad," he said, "it's the Stag Chase today. You'll be there, won't you?"

Dad grunted.

"You promised, Dad."

"Let me sleep," said Dad.

"That's all you do," said Ash. "Sleep and mess things up."

He slammed the door shut behind him.

Ash went downstairs, outside. He sat on the garden bench next to the wall, gazed with unfocused eyes above the trees to Tolley Carn, already smudged with heat.

Mom came out and sat down next to him. "I thought we could go for a drive. Then I'll drop you off in the village in time for the race."

Ash shook his head. "I don't want to go."

"For a drive or to the race?"

"Both."

"I know you're disappointed, sweetheart. But you'll regret it if you don't run. Probably for the rest of your life."

"I don't care."

"Yes, you do. You've spent months training for this. And

I know Dad hasn't gotten his act together yet today, but he's so proud of you. He'll be there when you race. I know he will."

"How do you know?"

"Because I know how much he loves you."

Ash sighed. He only hoped she was right. "Okay," he said. "You win."

"I win an hour in a car with a sulky teenager," she said, making a face at him. "Great."

He smiled in spite of himself.

They went out along the mountain roads. Mom didn't talk and Ash watched through the window as the land scrolled past like film scenery—mountains and valleys carved by vast forces of ice, water, wind, sculpted over billions of years. So ancient it seemed they must have been there always, must have always looked like this. But Ash knew the land owed its very form to change, to the slow forces of the elements that shaped it. Nothing stayed the same forever, not really. Not people, not families, not even the land itself. All you could do was hold on as best you could.

They stopped on the road halfway up Owl Cry Ridge, got out of the car, sat on a patch of scratchy brown grass. The breeze was cool against Ash's skin.

"Feeling any better now?" said Mom.

Ash nodded. "Yeah. A little."

"He'll be okay, you know. Your dad. It'll take time and there'll be ups and downs, but he'll get there."

"Do you really believe that?"

She smiled and shrugged. "Most of the time."

Ash watched a distant kestrel pause in the sky, then drop like a stone into the heather. "Why?" he said. "Why him? I don't get it. Other soldiers come home and they're fine."

"Some soldiers come home in body bags," said Mom. "Some come home with arms or legs missing, or in wheelchairs. Your dad came home with post-traumatic stress disorder. There's no why about it. Some soldiers get it and others don't. Everyone reacts differently to traumatic experiences."

"He jumps at shadows all the time," said Ash. "It's like he's scared of everything."

Mom sighed. "Your dad is one of the bravest men I know."

"Maybe he used to be," said Ash. "But he's changed. It's like he's a completely different person now."

Mom was quiet, gazing across the valley into the distance, something frozen and faraway in her expression.

"PTSD can come and go. With help, counseling, maybe medication for a while . . . it can be manageable. People can recover and lead normal lives."

"I keep getting angry with him," said Ash. "I know he can't help it, I know he's sick, but I still keep thinking that if he wanted to, if he really loved us, he'd get better. He'd get help. Or he'd at least try. But he isn't trying. He just shuts himself up in his room and I don't know what to do."

"I don't think there's anything you can do," said Mom. "Just run your race and then we'll take things one day at a time."

Ash looked out over the horizon. For the moment, everything looked at peace. No ghosts, nothing threatening.

Mom got to her feet. "Come on. We should head back."

Ash nodded, stood up.

"Is there anything you'd like to do before the race starts?"

Ash thought for a moment. "Yeah," he said. "I want to go to the cemetery."

Mom raised her eyebrows. "The cemetery? What for?"

"Well, because Tom Cullen saved Dad's life when Dad was the stag boy. It just feels like something I should do, before the race. Pay my respects."

But it was more than that. Tom Cullen's death was the reason Mark was running with ghosts and making crazy threats to kill the stag boy. His father was at the heart of everything Mark had done, everything Mark would do, and yet he was dead and gone—an absence around which chaos swirled. Ash wanted to stand at his grave. He needed Tom Cullen to be just Mark and Callie's dad again, just Dad's best friend again. A real person who had lived and died.

The main street was closed when they got there. Traffic cones and detour signs stood at either end to keep out cars. A crowd was already gathering, a mix of locals and tourists. People were setting up food stalls and souvenir stalls decked out with T-shirts, baseball caps, mugs and key rings, all bearing the stag's-head emblem. The new local economy, selling junk to tourists looking for a bit of Merrie Olde England.

They left the car on the side of the road and walked toward the cemetery. Through the gate, under the wooden arch, along the stone path that wound among the graves. Ash stopped at the one marked for Tom Cullen. He hadn't been there since the funeral and then it had just been a deep trench, earth scattering down onto the coffin, flowers and wreaths on the ground all around. Now there was a shiny rectangle of polished granite with gold lettering cut and painted into it. *Beloved father and husband.* There were still flowers on the grave, withered and dry, their colors faded.

"I was scared of him," said Ash. "He never smiled. He hardly ever spoke except to tell us what to do."

"He wasn't always like that," said Mom. "He used to be really fun. A bit wild until he married Ella and they had kids. He loved being a dad. He took Mark and Callie all over the mountains, taught them about wildlife and nature. He knew the name of every plant and every bird and bug. Your dad used to say Tom knew the name of every pebble too. Then Ella got sick."

Ash had a brief flash of a dark-haired woman with laughter in her eyes. "I don't remember her very well," he said. "Just what she looked like."

"Mark was only eight when she died so you must have been seven. It seems like such a long time ago. Tom was heartbroken and all alone out there with two young kids to look after and a farm to run. He kind of withdrew. He wouldn't accept any help, but he should have. He needed it. The kids needed it. I guess by the time the foot-and-mouth hit, he was already at his breaking point. He didn't have anything left for another crisis."

Ash nodded. He gazed down at the dead flowers and

noticed there was something tucked in among them, catching the sunlight. He crouched and picked it up. A card inside a clear plastic sleeve. He turned it over.

It was a small photograph, one he'd never seen before. He recognized the setting right away, though: the upper slope of Stag's Leap. It was a sunny day and Tom Cullen was standing with a dark-haired little girl on his shoulders, her hands clamped over his eyes. They were both laughing. Next to him, smiling broadly, stood Ash's own dad, and in front of them were two small boys. Mark, sturdy and brown and smiling. And Ash, slimmer and more serious, looking up at Mark.

"What's that?" said Mom.

He showed her the photograph. "Were you there as well?"

"I would think so," she said. "When your dad was home on leave, we sometimes used to take picnics up there with you kids. Ella was always taking pictures. This must be one of hers."

Ash tucked the photograph back among the dead flowers.

They walked slowly back to the road.

"You go and do whatever it is you have to do before the race starts," said Mom. "I'll go home. See what's going on. I'll make sure your dad is there to watch you run. I promise."

Ash nodded. He watched her walk back to the car, wave, drive away.

Then he drew a long breath and headed for the starting point—the Huntsman Inn.

26

THERE WAS A TV CREW in front of the inn. The camera trained on a shiny-faced reporter sweating in suit and tie, adjusting his smile. "Today I'm in Thornditch for the historic Stag Chase," he said. Then he said it again and again, as if he was stuck on Loop.

Ash slipped past the TV crew into the parking lot next to the inn. Flags were strung between the trees. Starlings squabbled in the treetops. The air was already glassy with heat. Outside the inn, folk dancers leaped and turned and clacked sticks like swords. Bells jangled below their knees. A man dressed in a shaggy costume of foliage skipped chaotically around them, then stopped and lifted his arms like branches. He stared in Ash's direction, eyes bright and curious behind a leafy mask.

At the edge of the crowd, the hound boys prowled. They were already decked out in their long black shorts, vests, masks of paint-stiffened cloth. They struck poses for photographers. Howled and strutted for attention.

Rupert Sloper, the Master of Hounds, came around the side of the pub. Quick, anxious movements. His belt sat high and tight around his potbelly. His round pink face shone with sweat. He scanned the crowd, the hound boys, until he spotted Ash. He waved and hurried over. "There you are!" he said. "You're late. I was starting to think you weren't coming."

"I know," said Ash. "Sorry."

Sloper stared at him, annoyed.

"Family stuff," said Ash. "I couldn't get away."

Sloper's expression softened. "Ah. I see."

Ash looked away. It seemed like everyone knew about his father.

Sloper cleared his throat. "I trust everything is all right now."

Ash shrugged. "I'm here, aren't I?"

"Yes, yes, you are," said Sloper. "Good. Well, this way, then."

He led Ash through a side door, along a gloomy corridor, into a small windowless room that smelled of stale beer. A bare lightbulb gave off a harsh white glare. A table and a couple of chairs stood in one corner. A blotched mirror hung on the wall.

"Your kit's on the table. I'll wait outside the door while you get changed, then I'll need to brief you about your destination."

The secret destination, known only by the Master of Hounds and soon Ash as well, but not the hound boys.

Ash pulled on black knee-length shorts and a dull reddish-brown runners' vest. Then the half-mask, made of stiffened cloth, pale brown smudged with black in rough approximation of a stag's face. No antlers. He'd get to wear the antler headdress only if he won the race.

169

Last was a small backpack. Inside it were two bottles of water, a few energy bars, a tiny compass, Band-Aids, a whistle for emergencies, an ordnance survey map.

Ash's reflection gazed back at him from the mirror. In the mask, he seemed only partly himself. The other part was already the stag: wild, fearful, exhilarated.

He went back out into the corridor where the Master of Hounds was pacing and waiting.

"All set?" said Sloper.

Ash nodded. He watched Sloper through the eyeholes in the mask.

"Right then. It's almost time. Ready for your briefing?"

"Yeah," said Ash.

Sloper glanced back, checking no one else was around to overhear. "Your destination is Black Crag. If you don't know where it is, check the map in your pack. It's marked on there."

"I know where it is."

"Okay. Good. At the summit of Black Crag, there's a cairn. It's a stack of stones, sort of cone shaped, not quite as tall as you. Lift the top stone and in the hollow underneath you'll find a pendant with a leather string threaded through it. Put it around your neck and then get back here without getting caught by the hounds. If they catch you, you've lost and the race is over but you still have to come back here and check in so we know that you've made it back. That clear?"

"Yes," said Ash. "Head for Black Crag, retrieve the pendant from the cairn, get back here."

"Simple enough," said Sloper. "Good."

Then came the safety briefing.

Drink plenty of water. There'll be extra on Black Crag, if you need it.

Stay within the circle marked in red on the map. Don't go beyond the marker flags at the boundaries of the race area.

In the event of injury or getting lost, stay where you are. Blow the whistle once every two minutes and wait for the rescue team to locate you.

If you're not back by four p.m., rescue teams will be sent out automatically.

"Don't take risks," said Sloper. "We don't want any broken bones or dead bodies."

Too bad no one was giving Mark a safety briefing, Ash thought. But instead he said, "I'll be careful."

"Good lad. The horn will sound at ten sharp." Sloper checked his watch. "You've got about ten more minutes. You'll set off first. Then you've got thirty minutes to get as far away as you can before the horn sounds again and the hounds set off after you."

Ash nodded.

"Ready?" said Sloper.

"Ready."

He followed Sloper out into the bright sunlight. The hound boys circled and bayed, a wild excited ululation. They kept their distance, followed Ash with their eyes as they paced, already moving like predators.

Ash's stomach tightened.

They're just boys, he told himself. Boys in stupid masks. But they were more than that, he knew. Not just boys anymore but actors in an ancient drama played out year after year for centuries. They were hounds and he was the stag boy, and they would do everything in their power to hunt him down.

But he would do everything in his power to stay ahead of them.

Beyond the rope barriers, he glimpsed a girl he thought was Callie and half raised his hand to her but the throng milled around her and she was gone.

He scanned the crowd again for Mom and Dad.

No sign of them anywhere.

Disappointment hollowed his chest. All this work and effort, all those months of training, and Dad nowhere in sight. There was no point in running the race if Dad wasn't there to see it, wasn't there to meet him at the finish line. Ash might as well rip off the mask, walk away, go home, go out into the mountains, go anywhere but here.

The hound boys yowled and paced and panted.

Beyond them, onlookers pointed cameras at him.

One of the hound boys came closer. He skirted Ash like a wolf. Head down. Long, slow strides. He looked different from the others. His mask was bone-white and bloodred. Arms, shoulders, legs streaked with charcoal and clay.

He stopped, stood with hands on hips and stared at Ash. Then he laughed.

Ash knew that laugh.

"Mark," he said.

Above the clamor of the hounds he heard Sloper's voice

over the PA system calling everyone to their places for the start of the race.

"You came, then," said Mark. "You're going to be the stag boy, even though I warned you not to. I gave you a chance. Whatever happens now, it's on your head."

"You're not going to kill me," said Ash. "Because you're not going to catch me."

Mark came closer, leaned in to him. His breath hot against Ash's ear. "We're going to tear you apart, Ash Tyler," he said. Then that singsong, whispery chant: "Earth and stone, fire and ash, blood and bone."

Ash shoved him, as hard as he could. Mark staggered back theatrically, then straightened. He stood there, eyes narrowed, mean. Then he turned away and went back among the circling hound boys, matching his pace and voice to theirs.

A musical blast ripped through the air, trailed off into a trembling wail. The hunting horn.

The crowd fell silent. All eyes on Ash.

And still no sign of Dad.

Tears burned hot in Ash's eyes. He might as well just walk away. They'd watch and mutter and wonder about his reasons, his lack of character. Sloper would trot after him, all in a frenzy and flustered, pleading with him. They'd blame him for ruining the day. But they couldn't stop him.

He could run away from the race, from home, from Mark, from all of it.

What then, Ash Tyler?

They'd get another boy to run, one of the hounds. Then maybe Mark really would go through with his plans, kill the stag boy in the belief that he could bring back his dad from the Otherworld. Ash could tell Mr. Sloper, warn him about Mark's threats. But no one would believe him. They'd think it was just the usual pre-Chase pranks, and Mark would laugh and agree with them and the Stag Chase would go ahead with or without him.

Besides, this was Ash's responsibility and he had trained to win. He was going to run this race for Dad, carry on the family tradition, even if Dad wasn't there to see him do it.

He drew a slow, deep breath. Squared his shoulders and crossed to the starting line. Stretched, hopped from foot to foot, shook the tension from his body.

Sloper touched his arm. "You remember what I told you and take care out there, lad. Three more blasts on the horn now and you're off."

Ash nodded.

The first blast sounded. The second.

The third.

27

ASH RAN.

His legs felt like jelly. His chest was so tight he couldn't catch his breath. The faces in the crowd blurred. The cheering, whooping and clapping morphed into white noise.

He ran out of the parking lot, along the main street, past Morris men and jugglers, hot dog stalls and an ice cream van and a stall selling stupid fake antlers attached to headbands.

The crowd thinned to nothing. Its clamor sank away. Ash pushed the mask back over his head so he could see properly. He heard the steady thump of his heart, the wild song of his blood, his own sharp, shallow breaths. Beyond these there was stillness, silence, space, and now he settled into his running, strong and steady.

He ran under the wooden arch that led into the cemetery, past Tom Cullen's grave, past the gnarly yew tree and a bramble-grown corner. Then he ducked through a leafy tunnel in the tall beech hedge and came out into bright sunlight. He chased the long shadow of himself along the footpath through the fields to Tolley Carn, ran around it, skirted the mountain lake. After he'd run past the lake, he headed into the folds of mountain and valley beyond. This was where he'd throw the hounds off his trail, lose them among the creases and dips and humps of the lower slopes, hide in the gullies and behind rock stacks and crags. He'd keep to the little tracks, half-hidden by gorse and bracken, stay below the skyline.

Ash was fast. He was silent. He was stealthy as a fox.

He headed west, along one of the faint and ancient footpaths spun like cobwebs over the land. He slithered down a slick patch of grass to a dry streambed. Ran between ranks of tall reeds with seed heads like loose cotton-wool balls. The air felt as thick and warm as soup.

In the distance behind him rose the thin wail of the hunting horn. The hound boys would be setting off now, running at full speed to catch up with him before he got too deep into the wild land.

Instinctively Ash picked up his pace.

He followed the streambed until it stopped at a wall of rock. Usually there was a waterfall here, a narrow torrent of clear cold mountain water that plunged into a seething pool. Now there was only a trickle and a slimy height with a stagnant greenish pool at its foot. Water bugs skating on its surface. Tiny flies storming above it.

He scrambled up the bank to the side of it, gorse ripping at his skin.

Ahead, Black Crag loomed against the skyline.

Ash paused in a shady hollow to catch his breath. Somewhere far behind him the hound boys would be fanning out, searching, trying to work out his route and his destination.

He left the streambed and crossed a desert of sharp black stones spiked with dead brown weeds. Sweat crawled down his face.

Black Crag, as raw as a mountain of the moon. Slopes of black scree, rock, burned wiry grass. A faint path slashed its way to the summit in full view of anyone looking up from the valleys and ridges below. Everything else was a climb or a slither. There was no choice but to take the path.

Speed, then, if he couldn't hide. It was too steep and unstable to run here, but he climbed fast. His breath sawing in and out. Sweat glittering on his skin. A knot of pain tightening in his right calf. He'd stretch it out when he found a hidden spot to grab a few moments of rest.

Up here, the wind was stronger and colder, respite from the heavy summer heat. By the time he was halfway up, the sun was no more than a white blur behind thickening gray clouds.

Ash passed a gorse bush sculpted by the wind into a sideways teardrop, its yellow flowers bright as flames. The path led between two tall stones leaning drunkenly toward each other. Beyond those, a torrent of scree lay between him and the peak. He started across it. Rock fragments skittered behind him and clacked their way down the mountain. He clambered over rock now, thick weatherworn slabs untidily piled on top of one another. Ahead lay a craggy climb to the stacked stones of the cairn.

Below, mountain and valley stretched away into deepening murk. It wasn't eleven o'clock in the morning yet, but already it was as gloomy as dusk.

Summer coming to an end, today of all days.

Ash stopped to catch his breath and ease out the knot in his calf. On the mountainside across the valley, three figures picked their way up a steep path.

Hound boys.

Ash froze. He was out in the open, against the skyline. He cursed softly. They'd see him right away if they glanced in his direction. Slowly he lowered himself into a crouch, then inched behind the nearest jag of rock. He peered around it. The hound boys were still trudging along the path, tiny figures moving in single file.

He watched them until they vanished around the side of the mountain.

They didn't seem to have seen him. Ash was safe, for now. But he had to be more careful, keep a lookout, stay down low where there was less chance of being spotted.

He eyed the climb to the summit. It was exposed, shelterless. Nowhere to hide if there were more hound boys moving through the nearby mountains.

He'd just have to risk it.

There was no path here, only a steep ascent over fissured jags of rock, sharp and gritty against his skin. He hauled himself upward by his fingertips and toes.

At last Ash pulled himself over the top, lay panting on a patch of hard dirt in the shade of the cairn.

He stood up, still breathing hard, and hefted away the cairn's top stone. It was heavier than he expected, a smooth weight that slipped through his fingers and clacked noisily down the slope. He froze. If the hound boys he'd seen earlier were still somewhere nearby, they'd surely have heard it. He looked around, listened.

Silence. No sign of any movement.

They must have moved on.

Ash was okay.

He fumbled in the hollow where the top stone had been. And there was the pendant, just as Sloper had said it would be. Ash lifted it out. A leather cord threaded through a polished disk cut from an antler. The stag's-head emblem burned into both sides.

He put it around his neck. Now it was his. But retrieving the pendant was the easy part. The difficult task was what came next: making it back to Thornditch before the hound boys caught up with him. By now, they'd have spread out through the valleys and mountains. They'd be scouring the slopes for any sign of the stag boy. If any of them spotted him, the cry would go up and they'd all come running.

The time for speed was over. From now on, it was stealth that mattered most.

First Ash needed a few moments of rest. He sat down on a flat rock with his back against the cairn. Stretched and flexed his legs until the cramp in his calf loosened. His breathing slowed, heart rate too.

At eye level, a buzzard circled in the darkening sky, then veered off southward, toward the shelter of valley and woodland.

A few fat drops of rain hit his face and arms. He looked up, hardly believing it. After nearly three months of drought, rain. Ash lifted his face, tasted drops on his tongue. It was real, rain falling harder and faster now. Soon the parched mountain streams would run with water again. There'd be green in the valleys instead of browns and dull golds. The bad times were over. The land would heal. It was going to be all right.

Ash raised his arms to the sky. Rain falling in glittering chains. Suddenly he felt giddy with excitement, the Stag Chase momentarily forgotten as he laughed and spun in the downpour. The rain washed the sweat and dust from his skin.

Clouds piled in from the north. The wind moaned over the rocks.

He looked toward the horizon, and the clouds blotted out the sun.

Abruptly, Ash stopped his joyful dance.

28

THE GLOOM LEACHED COLOR FROM the land. Grayed the scorched grass, dulled the bracken, tarred the rocks with shadow.

Along the eastern horizon a line of enormous boulders hunched like giant crouching beasts under the angry sky.

Shivering with cold, Ash started back down Black Crag.

Halfway down, his feet skidded on a patch of loose stone and suddenly the ground beneath him was moving. Arms flailing, he clawed at the air, then lost his balance completely. He tumbled down in a gritty torrent of stones and dirt until a clump of spiky gorse bushes broke his fall. The long needles stabbed into his hand. He scrambled free, stood and pulled needles one by one from his flesh. Beads of blood welled out. Fear ran through him, as if the scent of his blood might bring predators hungering along his trail.

As if in reply, the sighing wind carried the distant baying of the hound boys to him. He stopped to listen, uneasy, wondering if these were real boys or wraiths. Either way, they must have seen him. Ash's heartbeat quickened. Now the chase was really on.

The wind drove the rain into him. Thunder growled. A

few seconds later, lightning ripped through the gathering dark.

Ash set off again, followed a path around the shoulder of the mountain, out of sight of the hounds. He descended more slowly now, placed his feet carefully. He reached a short drop. If there were any boundary flags here to stop him from going this way, he missed them in the gloom. He eased over the edge, hooked his fingers into crevices, pressed himself against stone already slippery with rain. Felt around for toeholds, descended a little farther. Halfway down he lost his grip. He landed awkwardly, banged his ankle against a knuckle of rock. He rubbed it, tested his weight on it. Bruised but nothing broken, nothing sprained.

Even so, there was no path here. There was only a dense scrub of heather and gorse, bracken and stunted thorn trees.

Ash glanced back up toward the summit. In the storm light, Black Crag looked different. Not transformed exactly but somehow more than itself, its features taken to extremes. Its southern flank rose to its blunt summit in rocky jags, like the hackles of a hyena. Then it dropped down to the north in a series of huge steps.

The hound boys bayed again, closer this time, their calls echoed by other boys scattered through the nearby mountains and valleys. They were the hunters and Ash was the hunted. Suddenly he felt sick with fear.

Breathe. Think.

The rain slanted in—sheets of it—gray and cold.

Without a path to follow, the going was rough. Ash's feet

sank into the thick mattress of scratchy heather. Already the skin around his ankles felt raw. But he lumbered on, wading through the dense growth, moving from one rocky island to the next.

The rain changed. It became thinner and harder. It stung like grit on his exposed skin. His soaked vest and shorts clung uncomfortably to his body.

At last Ash came to another path. It was faint, the merest trace, a path worn not by people but by generations of grazing sheep, and leading nowhere in particular. But at least it was a path. Head down under the tilted mask, he ran along it, down into the valley and around Midsummer Tor to where the western end of Stag's Leap rose like a vast petrified wave from the valley floor.

The wind picked up then, hammered Ash with hard howling gusts. Rain swept across the land. It bounced off the rock, off sunbaked mud, off patches of grass, exploded into a fine mist. Raindrops glittered in his eyelashes.

He heard faraway voices again. Figures moved through the blur of rain. Ash hid in the bracken, watching them through a lattice of fronds. Three of them, hound boys, walking in single file. Flesh-and-blood boys, solid and steady—as far as Ash could tell.

They came out onto the open ground and stopped. Ash froze, held his breath. Any moment now they'd look his way, see him hiding there, bedraggled and pathetic.

The wind carried their voices.

"Are you sure you saw him? You're sure he came this way?"

"He must have. There's nowhere else he could go without us seeing him. He must be up on the Leap somewhere."

"Can't see a damn thing in this rain. We should have run faster. We should have got to him before the storm started."

"He can't have gone far. Running into that wind's like running into a wall."

"He's probably hiding around here somewhere, crawled into a hole or behind a rock or something."

Ash froze. If they started searching, it wouldn't take them long to find him.

"Split up," said one of them. "Scout around."

Ash hunkered down farther, a tight ball in a thicket of bracken. He heard one of them blunder toward him, singing under his breath. *"Hush, little stag boy, don't you cry . . ."* The hound boy stopped and stood so close that Ash imagined he could feel the heat from his body, hear the raindrops hitting his skin.

Ash closed his eyes. *If I can't see him, then he can't see me.*

All at once, the hound boy turned and crashed away.

Ash opened his eyes, peered through the bracken again.

They were standing together about ten yards away. He could hear the urgency in their voices but he couldn't make out their words. Then one of them gestured down the mountainside. A few seconds later they headed off, loping along like wolves following the scent trail of their prey.

Ash huddled in the hard rain, shivering, blinking water from his eyelashes.

When he was sure they were too far away to see him if they looked back, he stood up.

The hound boys were lost to the rain haze but they were still out there somewhere, most likely seeking others to help them search.

Being stealthy would only get him so far. Now he'd have to move fast as well.

Ash had climbed the northern slope of the Leap with Dad at least a dozen times. It was a slog but straightforward enough, no need for ropes. Even in the sheeting rain, he climbed steadily.

At the top, he stopped. In the storm gloom, he was no longer afraid that the hound boys would see him. He could run the length of the ridge, descend along the path that dropped down past the Cullen farm to the valley, loop around and return to Thornditch from the east.

He set off at a steady trot, stones clacking underfoot, mud splattering up his legs.

He ran half a mile along the ridge. He was breathing easier now, hitting his stride, each step bringing him closer to the finish line.

Then, through the welter of the storm, a figure came toward him.

A HAZY SHADOW AT FIRST, featureless. Then, as the figure came closer, Ash could make out more detail. The ragged outline of a hound mask. A muscular body streaked with pale clay, moving with an unhurried stride toward him, head lowered, arms swinging a little, loose and dangerous.

A warrior's walk, not a hunter's.

Mark.

No point in running now.

Mark stopped a few feet away, facing Ash. Watched him from behind his mask.

"You're bleeding," said Mark. "I can smell it. That's how I found you. I followed the scent of your blood and it led me straight to you."

"Don't talk like that," said Ash. "You're not a real hound, you're a boy."

Mark laughed. "It would be good, though, wouldn't it? Tracking you down by the scent of your blood."

"So then how did you find me?"

"I knew you'd come to the Leap."

"You can't have known. Even I didn't know."

"And yet here you are."

They stared at each other. "What now?" said Ash.

But he already knew the answer. He was caught. His Stag Chase was over. All that training, everything he'd gone through, it was all for nothing. Ash wouldn't cross the finish line in triumph, wouldn't get to wear the antler headdress. Even if Mom got Dad to leave the house and brought him to the race, there'd be no victory to celebrate. No win to share with Dad, to help bring Dad out of the dark head space he'd been in ever since he got home.

Ash felt like he didn't even care anymore. It was over. He'd failed.

He took off the stag's head pendant from around his neck and held it out to Mark. "Take it. I'm done. I'm going home."

"I don't want it."

"I'm not looking for favors. You caught me, fair and square. You win and I lose. Take it."

"You still don't get it, do you?" said Mark. He wrenched off his mask and hurled it into the screaming wind. "I don't care about the stupid pendant. I don't care who wins the race. That's not what it's about."

"I know it's not," said Ash. "But it should be. We could just do what we're supposed to do. You could take the pendant, go back down there to Sloper, be a hero. And I could just go home."

"You know I can't let that happen." Mark gazed away, into the gloom. "My dad, he never should have died. It wasn't his time. It was a mistake. And I have to make things right."

"By killing me? That's really what you've come here to do?"

Mark smiled, turned his back on Ash, opened his arms. "Don't you see them?" he said. "The wraiths? They're coming for you. The hound boys from the old days, from the dark times."

Ash looked away from Mark, beyond him, into the driving rain. Movement in its depths, blurry shadows advancing. A dozen or more of them, their movements erratic and unnatural. They leaped and twisted, flitted this way and that with a speed and lightness that no flesh-and-blood boy possessed.

The hairs on the back of his neck prickled. "What do they want?"

"They want you. They want blood and death."

"Why, though? What for?"

Mark smiled at him, cold and strange. "It's nothing personal. They're hounds and you're the stag boy. They hunt and kill. It's just what they do. It's all they know."

"So what are they? The ghosts of medieval psychopaths or something?"

Mark shook his head. "It's like I told you, in the old days if the hounds caught the stag boy, they'd kill him. A blood offering to the land. Centuries of blood and death and terror, the old ways written into the land, like memories. And when the land gets sick, like now, its ghosts wake and the old ways come back. People tried to forget them, but they won't be forgotten."

"How do you know all this?"

"Because the hill farmers refused to forget. They passed

it on, father to son, mother to daughter, down the generations. The land is part of my family history. My grandpa
told it to my dad and my dad told it to me. The past doesn't
go away, no matter how much people want it to. It's still all
around us."

Ash shivered, watching the dim shapes of the wraith
hound boys moving through the rain.

Mark came closer. Head down, skip, skip, from foot
to foot. "Out here, if you take something, you have to give
something back," he said. "It's the way of things. Once
upon a time, people knew that. That's what the stag boy
is supposed to be, a sacrifice to the land in times of hardship. Well, it's a time of hardship now, isn't it? The sheep all
slaughtered, the land diseased, hill farmers going bankrupt
and getting kicked off their land, my dad dead. Disease and
debt and death. Sometimes we have to go back to the old
ways to make things right. Blood for blood, life for life."
Mark stopped skipping, lifted his head. Eyes bright and
fierce behind the mask. "The stag boy's life in exchange for
my dad's."

The wraiths came closer through the murk. Baying,
yelping, howling.

Ash started to move away. "Your dad's dead," he said.
"Nothing's going to bring him back."

"Look around you," said Mark. "All those hound boys
are dead. But they've come back."

"No," said Ash. "They haven't come back, not really.
They're just ghosts. They're not alive like me and you. Is

that really what you want? You want your dad to be like one of those howling crazy ghosts out there?"

"Earth and stone needs blood and bone, Ash Tyler. It always has and it always will. It takes life so that it can give life. One life for another. I didn't want it to be you. I told you to pull out of the race. I tried to save you."

"Then what? You'd sacrifice some other kid instead of me? It's not right, Mark."

Mark took a step toward him. "I'll tell you what's not right. Losing my dad. I came out here into the mountains. I walked and walked. I didn't eat for days. I didn't sleep. I walked and I searched for answers or a sign or . . . something. Anything. And in the end the ghosts came to me from their dead place, hound boys from the ancient days. They were weak then, whispering voices and a breath of mist. But the longer they were around me and the more I let them into my head, the stronger they became. They whispered things to me. They told me to kill the birds."

"The birds?"

Mark nodded. "Bone Jack's crows. Kill the birds and take Bone Jack's power. Now he's the weak one, too weak to stop the dead from getting through. Bone Jack can't stop the hound boys. He can't stop me from bringing back my dad."

Ash shifted uneasily. "I've seen Bone Jack," he said. "I've spoken to him. He doesn't seem weak to me. He's ancient, magical, powerful. It will take a lot more than you killing a few crows to destroy him."

"You're wrong," said Mark. "He's losing control. That's how the hound boys could cross over from Annwn."

Ash remembered the wolf. That must have come through from the other side too. That was why Bone Jack had come for it. *Back . . . where he belongs,* he had said. What had he meant by that? Back into the past? Or back to Annwn, the Otherworld, perhaps? But the wolf hadn't been a wraith. It had felt real, solid. Ash had run his fingers through its fur, searching for a collar. He'd felt its ribs, felt its hot breath on his skin as he'd dribbled water into its mouth.

Maybe it was different with animals, or it had been dead a shorter time. Or maybe the hound boys weren't as wraith-like as they looked.

He switched his attention to Mark again. "If Bone Jack can't stop you from bringing back your dad, why don't you just go and get him?"

Mark shook his head at him. His eyes were wild, dangerous. "It won't work unless you die," he said. "I told you: life for life. I have to sacrifice the stag boy and defeat Bone Jack so the hounds can take me through to Annwn and I can bring back my father."

"Is that what the hound boys told you? And you're just going to do what they say? How do you know you can trust them?"

"They need me," said Mark. "And I need them."

Ash shook his head. There was no getting through to Mark. "Look," said Ash, "All I wanted was to run this race for my dad. That's it. Now you've caught me so it's over. Okay? It's over. Let's just go home, you and me together."

Ash backed away farther. But the ghost hound boys tore from the gloom, spun and lunged and soared. One of them hurtled past him. Ash felt the boy's cold airy touch against his skin, breathed in the ancient stink of the grave.

He flinched, shuddered. "Call them off, Mark," he said. "Please. Get them off me!"

Mark shook his head. "I can't. I don't tell them what to do, and it's not over just because you want it to be."

The hounds drew back into the rain, regrouped. Endlessly moving, shifting, advancing again, circling, crowding around Ash. They were in front of him, to his side, behind him. One moment they seemed like ordinary boys in masks, boys like him. The next they were wraiths, rags of mist veiling scorched bone, lipless grins, empty eye sockets.

Ash hurled himself in the only direction left open to him. Scrambled over scree, slipping on wet black stone as shiny as plastic. Across springy turf that squelched underfoot, on to rain-slick rock.

He glanced back. Mark was standing where he'd left him, watching him.

Ash ran harder, faster.

Again the spectral hound boys advanced through the rain. Still spinning and leaping but moving forward slowly, as if it didn't really matter that he'd bolted. As if they, like Mark, already knew that he was trapped.

Rain swept over the ridge. The wind screamed. And through it came Mark, and the wind's scream became his scream, and so too did the beating of Ash's heart and the pounding of his blood, all one squalling primal shriek.

Then suddenly, Mark flew at Ash. Smashed into him, seized him, beat him down onto rock and pooling rainwater.

Ash threw out wild panicky punches. He twisted free, rolled over, scrambled away on all fours. Too close to the edge of the Leap. He switched direction, away from the drop, then he got to his feet, winded and gasping for breath. But Mark wasn't done yet. He cannoned into Ash again, a low tackle that sent Ash reeling backward toward the edge again. Closer this time.

Ash screamed through the wind and rain.

But Mark came at him a third time. Again the impact shunted Ash backward. Then he realized. That was what Mark wanted, to push him back and back until he fell off the edge and flailed down onto the splintered rocks below.

Ash veered away from the edge. He stood gasping in the rain, head down, facing Mark. "Please. Don't do this," he said. "Your dad wouldn't want you to do this."

"You don't know what my dad would want."

"I do," said Ash. "I know. Those wraiths came after my dad when he was the stag boy twenty years ago. They got into his head and because of them he ended up on the Leap about to jump off. I don't know how but they made him want to jump. But your dad saw my dad standing there, right at the edge, and he pulled him back. He saved my dad's life."

"Liar!" screamed Mark. He came at Ash again. But this time Ash sidestepped, flung his arms around Mark, clung to him. They lurched and wrestled, a weird dance in the howling chaos of the storm.

"It's true," said Ash. The words came out like sobs. "It's true. And I know you don't really want to kill me. You're not a killer."

And then it stopped. Mark stopped. Let go of Ash. He stood there in the weltering storm, his chest heaving, his eyes bright with tears.

But the spectral hound boys came from behind, hurtling with the storm wind. Mark standing with his back to them, between them and Ash at the cliff edge. They hound boys kept coming, didn't stop. They smashed into Mark, then into Ash.

Ash staggered. Off balance, the world tilting, the wind battering around him. He felt Mark's hand close around his wrist, felt Mark brace and strain and use his weight to try to haul Ash back from the edge. But it was no use. There was nothing beneath his feet anymore. Ash plunged through the wild air, with Mark still holding on, the two falling together.

They hurtled downward, clawing at the rushing air. Then came the hard slam onto rock, a quake of pain, the taste of blood in his mouth, and a bottomless dark.

ASH OPENED HIS EYES AND stared straight up. The sky was churning with dark clouds. Rain spiking his face like nails.

For a few moments he had no idea where he was or what had happened.

Then he remembered falling.

He shifted his weight. Pain knifed in his shoulder. More pain in both elbows, his right hip, his head, his ribs. Everything ached. Was anything broken? Not his legs, not his arms, not his neck. Maybe his left shoulder. He couldn't tell. He only knew that it really hurt. Gritting his teeth, Ash hauled himself upright into a sitting position. He ran his fingers through his hair. The stag mask must have come off in the fall, torn away by the wind. His hand came away bloody.

But he was alive. Being dead couldn't hurt this much.

He'd landed on a ledge. Ahead was a short stretch of rain-glossed rock that tapered off to the right into a fifteen-foot high wall of rock. To his left, there were just a few inches of the ledge and then the drop.

No sign of Mark.

"*Please*," whispered Ash, his teeth chattering. "*Please don't let him have fallen all the way down.*"

A sob shook through Ash. He felt it, heard it, but it seemed to have nothing to do with him. A reaction of his body. His mind hadn't caught up yet.

What should he do?

You have to look, he told himself. You have to see if he's down there. Maybe there was another ledge, a slope, a mountain ash tree clinging to the rock face, anything that, by some miracle, might have broken Mark's fall.

Ash flattened himself against the ledge and inched forward.

Far below, splinters of black granite stabbed up through a sea of gloomy rain-mist.

There was no second ledge, no slope, no miraculous mountain ash, nothing that might have saved Mark. He must be down there somewhere in the cold murk, and he must be dead because no one could survive a fall like that, not even Mark.

Ash pushed himself back from the edge.

Only then did he look toward the other end of the ledge.

There, just a few feet away, was Mark.

Ash gasped with relief.

Mark was lying on his side with one arm twisted unnaturally beneath him. Eyes closed. His mouth slightly open. A trickle of blood, diluted by rainwater, ran down his forehead and dripped from the bridge of his nose.

He wasn't moving.

He looked dead.

Ash stared at him for a long time.

Then he crawled toward Mark. He tugged Mark's hand. It felt cold and limp, wet with rain. "Mark," he said. "Wake up, Mark. Come on, wake up."

Not a flicker of movement.

He pressed two fingers to Mark's throat to see if he had a pulse.

Nothing. He couldn't feel anything except Mark's chilled skin against his own. Then suddenly he felt a throb of life, faint but unmistakable.

"Come on, Mark. Wake up. Please."

Mark groaned, coughed, spat blood and rainwater. He rolled onto his back, then screamed with pain.

"Don't move," said Ash. "You're injured. I think your arm is broken. Maybe more."

Mark's breath came in quick dry gasps. "What happened?" he said. His voice was a whisper.

"The hound boys slammed into us. It was like being hit by the wind only much stronger. I was too close to the edge. I lost my balance. You tried to hold on to me but we both fell and landed on this ledge. We were lucky."

Ash shook in great slow shivers. Yet his thoughts were cold and clear, bright as ice now. They were trapped. Mark was injured. They were soaked to the skin and the storm was still raging and in these conditions the chances of a search party finding them by nightfall seemed tiny.

But they were alive.

For now.

He waited out the shivers.

When they stopped, he took off the backpack. He emptied its contents between his outstretched legs. Found the whistle and blew it. But the wind ripped away the thin sound. Even if anyone was out searching for them yet, they'd never hear the whistle in this storm.

Useless.

He slid the empty backpack under Mark's head as a pillow. Mark moaned, his eyes shut. Blood still trickling down the side of his face.

Ash sat with his back to the rock face. He drew up his knees, hugged himself into a tight ball. Rain beat on his skull, slid down his back, pooled underneath him. He stared into the murky distance. He was an ant, an atom. There was nothing he could do about anything anymore. The storm would rage. Night would come. If they survived until the morning, perhaps the search-and-rescue team would find them.

Perhaps.

Or else Mark might die.

Ash couldn't let that happen. No more running away.

But he couldn't go down the rock face, not without ropes and proper equipment. The drop was too far, sheer and hazardous.

Maybe he could climb back up to the top, get help.

He stood up. He walked the length of the ledge, feeling for handholds and footholds in the rock face. All he found were cracks too narrow to slide his fingers into, nubbins so smooth and slick with rain that his feet slithered off them right away.

Then he noticed an angle of rock sticking out, about a foot above his head. He jumped for it, reaching up with his good arm, fingers scraping the rock face a hand's breadth below it. Ash jumped again, and again, sobbing with the effort. But there wasn't enough strength left in him and he knew that even if he managed to reach it, he was too weak to pull himself up.

It was impossible.

He sank back down, defeated. He watched the endless fall of rain, drops shattering in diamond bursts on the rock in front of him. He watched dark clouds as tall as mountains heave and collide and tear apart. The brief brilliant burn of distant lightning.

Time passed. Ash wasn't sure how much or how quickly. He slept a little, woke with a start, slept again, woke. Whenever he woke, he glanced across at Mark but Mark lay with his eyes closed, motionless except for the slight rise and fall of his chest as he breathed in and out.

It was starting to get dark now. And it would get colder. Ash knew that without shelter or dry clothes, and with the storm wind ripping away their body heat, they were almost certain to get hypothermia and then it would all be over.

They'd die out here, alone on this wind-blasted ledge.

Ash struggled to keep his eyes open but his eyelids felt too heavy, the pull of sleep too strong.

When Ash woke again, there seemed to be a third person on the ledge, blurry through the slanting rain. A boy, sitting at the farthest end of the rock. An impossible stag boy with his hair in spikes, his face and arms streaked with white and black clay. A stag's head design covered his chest, antlers branching over and around his shoulders: painted or tattooed onto his skin. His face gleamed with pale clay and rain rolled down his cheeks like tears.

Ash closed his eyes and shook his head to clear away the image. When he opened them, the boy was still there.

"Why are you here?" said Ash. "What do you want?"

The stag boy was silent, watching him.

"I've seen you before," said Ash. "Up on the top, a couple of weeks ago, running from the hound boys."

The stag boy stared.

"You're dead, like them," said Ash. "Aren't you? You've been dead for centuries."

The wind snatched away his words. But, as if the stag boy had heard enough, he stood up. Still holding Ash's gaze. Then, slowly and deliberately, he turned to face the rock wall. He went closer to it. He reached up, hooked his fingers into a tiny fissure and started to climb.

"Come down," said Ash weakly. "It's too dangerous. It's impossible. Come back."

Then he realized what he was saying. Talking to a dream, warning a ghost. Nothing was dangerous for a ghost.

The stag boy kept reaching and climbing and Ash kept watching until the boy hauled himself over the top and disappeared from sight.

Gone.

Just a dream. Just a ghost. Or some sort of memory imprinted on the land. Maybe Mark was right and that's what ghosts were, Ash thought. Land memories, visual echoes of the past. Terrible things had happened out here and the land remembered. *Earth and stone, fire and ash, blood and bone.* Perhaps those that died became part of the land itself, its dreaming, its nightmares. And sometimes, when death stalked the mountains and valleys again and the soil was dark with blood and the people mad with despair, maybe the past broke through again, became a haunting.

Ash remembered the book he'd taken from Bone Jack's hut. The poem printed in it.

> I have been in a multitude of shapes,
> Before I assumed a consistent form.

Ash's thoughts jarred, jammed, broke apart. He raised his face to the darkening sky. Opened his mouth and tasted the rain.

> I will believe when it is apparent.
> I have been a tear in the air,
> I have been the dullest of stars . . .

Not a star in the sky now. Not one.
Get it together. Think. Move, Ash told himself.
He shook tears of rainwater from his eyes.

> I will believe when it is apparent.

What did that line in the poem mean? When *what* is apparent?

Something would be made clear, something he could believe in, that he could trust.

But what?

A memory flickered in his mind. He tried to catch it but it slipped away from him. Stop trying so hard, he told himself. Breathe softly, make your mind quiet. And through the quiet it came to him. A story he'd heard when he was a child and almost, but not quite, forgotten until now—a story about how, long ago, the hounds had chased the stag boy up onto the Leap. And the stag boy had fallen. Fallen and landed on the ledge, just like Ash.

And he'd climbed back up.

Suddenly he knew.

If the stag boy had climbed the rock face, that meant Ash could too.

Ash struggled to his feet. Shivering, stiff with cold. Every inch of his body felt battered and bruised. He stamped warmth back into his muscles, flexed and stretched. He quickly ate two of the energy bars, washed them down with bottled water.

He crouched next to Mark. "I'm going to climb up out of here," he told him. "I'm going to get help. And then I'll come back for you."

Mark's eyes opened a crack.

Then Ash walked over and stood where the stag boy had stood. The ledge was narrow here, no more than an arm's length between the rock face and the drop. He reached up where the stag boy had reached, found a fissure in the rock just big enough to hook his fingers onto. The way the stag boy had shown him, the way Dad had taught him. He searched for a toehold, found a small jag of rock, then a hollow for his other foot, then another handhold.

Ash's bruised shoulder knotted with pain as it took his weight. He grunted and ignored it, held on, reached up with his free hand for another crack in the rock. Then the wind slammed him against the rock face and tore at him. Ash clung on by his fingertips. The side of his face pressed against wet rock. Every sinew in his body strained. If he fell from here, there was no chance he'd land on the ledge again. He'd fall all the way down to the far-below rocks. He'd shatter.

His head spun with a horror of heights.

Ash held himself very still, concentrated on the rock face, steadied his breathing. When the wind had subsided a bit, he grabbed the next handhold, the next foothold. One by one.

On and on, up and up.

Then he reached up and there was no more rock, just air, and finally rough grass under his hand. He dug his fingers into wet gritty turf. Another heave and Ash was halfway over the edge of the Leap. He clawed at mud and loose stone. His fingers scraped through wet grass and he lost hold. He slid backward down the rock face a ways, pain searing through his shoulder again as he tried to cling on, feet scrabbling against the rocks for a toehold. Then he found one, shunted himself upward again. This time his hand closed around a tangle of thin roots. He clung on, pushed and pulled, hoped they wouldn't give way and tear from the soil.

Finally, Ash got one knee up on the edge and hauled himself over.

Limp as a rag, he lay on his back. Sharp stones dug into his ribs. He sucked air greedily, then rolled over, away from the edge. His eyes wide open. Skull full of the moan and boom of the wind.

The ghostly hound boys were nowhere in sight.

He laughed with relief.

He'd made it.

But it wasn't over yet. Mark was still down there, injured, perhaps even dying. Ash had to find help.

He got to his feet and stood swaying, squinting into the battering wind. In the far distance, the skyline glowed fiery red through the murk of rain. He frowned at it. Not sunset. This was different, a blazing line like a tide of lava flowing over the land toward him.

Weird, but still a long way off. There were more urgent things to worry about. He stumbled down the slope, as fast as he could. Twice he fell, knees cracking down on the rocky ground. But he hauled himself upright again, staggered on.

It was two miles back to Thornditch. The gloom thickening into dusk, the storm smashing against the mountains. Weak as Ash was, it could take him hours to get there. There was a good chance he wouldn't make it at all.

But there was nothing else he could do.

One foot in front of the other. Like Dad always used to say. Ash would crawl if he had to. He had to keep going.

But he was so tired, so weak. Exhaustion washed through him. Briefly he closed his eyes and immediately lost his balance. He staggered sideways, almost fell, righted himself.

Just then something moved farther down the slope. Ash stopped and peered through the rain. Now he saw them. Ghostly hound boys, as pale and ethereal as moonlight. They lifted their masked heads, sniffed the wind. Their eerie shriek-yelps rose above the storm.

He shivered with fear.

Too exhausted to run and nowhere to run to anyway.

Ash stood still and watched them come.

THEY CAME AT ASH LIKE a breaking wave. They raced and tumbled through the misty darkness. Their howls filled his ears, filled his skull until he couldn't think of anything else. Their bony fingers scraped over his skin. With each touch, he grew colder, weaker, until his trembling legs could no longer hold him upright and he sagged to the ground.

He knelt there in the hard rain.

"You're not real," he whispered to them. But they were. As real as the wolf, as real as the rocks and the storm.

Ash raised his head, peered into the rain. Ahead lay burned ground, leafless bone-white trees stark against a plain of blackened rock.

Not real. It couldn't be real.

Get up, said a voice.

He blinked rain from his eyelashes.

A whisper.

No one was there. The voice was in his head, nowhere else. He was alone.

Except for the ghostly hound boys.

Get up.

He pushed against the ground, against gravity, against the deadweight of his own body.

Get up, get up, the voice urged.

Ash pushed again. He stood swaying in the wind, head down, half-blinded by rain, looking out over a scorched landscape that should not be there. The distant rim of fire was fiercer now, getting closer all the time.

The hound boys circled, pressed in close again. He heard the click-clack of their bones, the moan of the wind through their fleshless skulls. The wind ripped trails of smoke from their grinning mouths.

The rain on his skin seemed as dark as blood. The air thick with smoke—bitter and foul.

And the rain kept falling.

Ash gathered up all his pain, all his fear, his exhaustion, because that was all that he had left, that was the sum of him—the brief, raw strength of despair. And then he charged straight into the hound boys. They lunged around him, blocked his path and his vision, clawed at him. But he kept going, felt them crunch and fold, then surge around him again, and still he kept going.

Then suddenly he was through them, out into the open.

Along the skyline, a wall of fire raced toward them.

Wildfire.

Not real, not real. None of this is real.

Around him the hound boys yapped and bayed.

Ash froze. His gaze fixed on the wildfire. A thorn tree exploded into flames. Dark smoke and gritty ash swirled in the wind. It raked his throat, brought stinging tears to his eyes. He coughed and retched.

None of this is real.

Or was it? After all, if the smoke could choke him, then surely the fire could burn him.

Suddenly he was seized by panic. Ahead lay the inferno, racing across the land, burning everything in its path, and behind him the slope rose steeply to the sheer drop of Stag's Leap. He was trapped.

Unless he could somehow climb back down to the ledge where Mark was. Maybe on the ledge they'd be safe from the fire.

Ash started to run, stumbling over the lumpy ground, slow, so slow, because there was no strength left in him, nothing keeping him on his feet now except raw terror.

Halfway back up to the top, he switched direction, cut across toward the cliff top where he and Mark had fallen.

Instantly the pack of spectral hound boys came after him. They clamored and swarmed, blocked Ash's path again. He veered away but they flowed around him, blocked him once more. He yelled and swung wild blows at them, but he was too exhausted, too weak.

This time they didn't fold and fall back, didn't let him through.

"Why are you doing this?" he said. Teeth chattering with fear and cold. His smoke-roughened voice no more than a whisper. "What do you want?"

They were silent behind their masks but he knew the answer in all its terrible simplicity: they wanted to kill him, the stag boy, and there was nothing more to them than this one overwhelming urge. There could be no pleading with them; there was nothing he could offer them.

In the distance beyond the hounds, fire raced between the dirty sky and the dark land.

The wind blew hot.

Ash sank to his knees. Nowhere to run. No strength left. Nothing he could do except wait for the wildfire to roll over him. Wait to die.

He gazed into a blazing shimmer of orange heat.

Suddenly something moved in its depths.

Something as black as shadow, moving fast, swift and low. It reached the fire line, bunched and bounded clear.

Ash rubbed tears and grit from his eyes, peered past the hounds, through the smoke and fire-flung shadows.

The wolf.

It leaped onto a boulder and stood stock-still. Impossibly, it seemed strong and healthy, a far cry from the dying beast he'd found in the mountains a few days ago. Yet it was undoubtedly the same animal. It watched him with bright amber eyes, its head lowered.

Behind it came a wild figure, untouched by the flames, striding out over the scorched ground, through smoke and storm. Long coat snapping out in the wind, gaunt face etched in shadow under his wide-brimmed hat. Eyes full of murder.

Bone Jack.

Ash blinked and stared, half-blinded by smoke. Now the raw cries of crows filled his ears. Dark within dark, against a spitting wall of flame. The wind shrieked.

Earth and stone, fire and ash, blood and bone.

As one, the hounds turned their dead faces toward Bone Jack.

Wild man, raggedy man, birdman.

Ash wanted to run, from the hounds, from the wildfire, from Bone Jack. Death was all around him but he couldn't move, couldn't even look away.

All he could do was watch.

In the blink of an eye, Bone Jack whirled, then shattered. Broke apart into wing, feather, beak until there was no longer any semblance of a man there, only crows, dozens of them, like black rags against the bright screen of wildfire. They tumbled and swooped. With every wing beat, every thrust of beak and claw, every serrated cry, they drove the hound boys back down the slope toward the flames.

The hounds howled, flailed at the birds.

But the birds kept coming.

Smoke gathered like a dense dark fog, sparking with fire as it rolled up the slope and over the hounds. Now the hounds flickered like shadows within it, the parched grass igniting beneath them. Flames danced up their tattered clothes, their clay-spiked hair. Briefly they whirled there, scarecrows of fire and blackened bone with charred grins, smoke misting all around them. Then the wall of flame collapsed over them and the hounds were gone.

At last Ash let out a sigh of relief. Coughs heaved up out of him. His eyes were raw with smoke.

Suddenly, the crows flew back out of the fire. They hurtled toward one another, flocked into a fluid shadow that darkened and deepened and shrank, shaping itself into a single solid form: Bone Jack, whole again, striding through swirling smoke with the wildfire rearing behind him and the wolf at his side.

Then Ash saw someone else, a little way up the slope, pale in the deepening darkness. Ash froze, squinting through the smoky gloom. One of the wraith hound boys. He must have escaped the flames and come back to finish the job. Finish Ash.

The gritty wind gusted, the smoke cleared a little, and now Ash saw that the figure wasn't one of the hounds.

It was the stag boy.

He was pacing, head down. Four quick strides out, sharp turn, four quick strides back. He stopped, watched Ash through his mask.

Bone Jack returned from the shadows then, moving fast, his gaze locked on the stag boy.

"You've got to go now," Ash called to the stag boy. "Go on, run. Get away."

The stag boy paced. One, two, three, four, turn. And now the wolf paced with him, shadowed him, matched him step for step.

"Run!" Ash yelled. But it was too late. Bone Jack was already there, spinning out wild nets of bird and shadow.

The stag boy stopped pacing. He stared at Bone Jack. "Come on, lad," said Bone Jack.

The stag boy leaned into the wind, took a step forward.

"Not him!" Ash yelled to Bone Jack. "He saved my life! He's not one of them!"

Another step. The stag boy was now airy as a ghost.

"Time to go home," said Bone Jack.

The stag boy already dissolving like mist, the dark land visible through him, the black wind howling around him. He reached out his hand toward Bone Jack and Bone Jack took it in his own, pulled the spectral stag boy to him, embraced him.

Then the boy was gone. No one there except Bone Jack, striding again toward Ash through the churning smoke, the wildfire bright as a furnace behind him.

Ash sagged to the ground. No strength, no hope, nothing. "What have you done?" he whispered. "Why? Why did you have to take him back?"

Bone Jack crouched in front of him. "Hush now, lad," he said.

"What have you done to him?" Ash said. "Is he dead?"

"He's been dead for centuries," said Bone Jack. "They all have. They've all got to go back."

"So why didn't you take them back days ago? Then none of this would have happened."

"Ain't that simple."

"Why not? Because Mark killed the crows?"

"Not that."

"What, then?"

"You ever tried catching mist with your bare hands? The hounds are like that. Most years they stay that way. Then, like mist, they fade to nothing in the morning sun. Death and drought made them strong this year. I had to wait until the Stag Chase so they'd be at their strongest, until they had weight and substance and they'd run you to the ground. Only then could I make things right, take them back where they belong. Sometimes you have to let things run their course before you make your move."

"You got them, though, in the end."

"Aye, I did."

"So what happens now?"

"Hush, lad. You've got to get up, get moving. You've got to get help for your friend."

Ash got to his feet, stood swaying in the storm.

"The storm's blowing the wildfire westward," said Bone Jack. "So stay on this path, come down the eastern side of the Leap."

Through the sheeting rain, Ash watched the tide of fire hunger along the mountainsides, hellish and unstoppable.

"How can there be rain and fire at the same time?" he whispered, half to himself.

"Because the land's so dry. Deep-down dry. Once wildfire's got a hold, it's as hot as a thousand furnaces. Evaporates the rain before it even hits the ground. It takes more than a few hours of rain to stop a wildfire."

Ash turned around to ask Bone Jack how he knew all this, but Bone Jack was gone and so was the wolf. No sign they'd ever even been there.

Ash was alone.

He took one step forward, then another.

ASH WALKED BUT NOTHING WORKED anymore. His legs were stone-heavy. He could barely lift his feet clear of the rough ground. The land lurched sideways. He slumped down onto the wet grass and lay there, too exhausted to get up again. He could lie here, he could close his eyes, he could drift away, sleep or die.

Then shouts below. A familiar voice.

Ash lifted his head.

Dad, running out of the wind and rain.

"Go back," Ash said. The words a whisper, sticking in his raw throat. "Go back down, Dad. There's wildfire. There's ghosts. It's not safe."

But Dad couldn't hear and Ash knew he wouldn't have turned back even if he could. He kept coming.

The blinding white glare of a flashlight. Ash flinched, turned his face away. And all at once Dad was there with him, holding him so tight it hurt, Dad shaking as much as Ash was.

"He was here," whispered Ash. "Bone Jack was here. And they've all burned and he's gone into the night."

"Who's burned? Who's gone?"

"The hound boys. They all burned in the wildfire. Dad, we need to get off the mountain. We need to get help."

"No one burned," said Dad. Voice taut as wire. "The hound boys all came back into town. Only you and Mark Cullen are missing. And I've got you now. It's going to be all right."

But Ash wasn't so sure. "We fell off the Leap," said Ash. "We landed on a ledge. Mark's injured. I climbed up to get help."

"How bad is he?"

"I don't know. I think his arm is broken, and he banged his head. I left him about an hour ago, I think, to get help. He was unconscious but he was still alive."

Dad swore. His voice jittery, full of panic.

Ash looked at Dad. His voice shaking as much as his body, he said, "Dad, we have to help Mark. We can't just leave him there on that ledge."

"You're right," said Dad. "We won't." He drew a long, slow breath, squared his shoulders. "But first things first." He took off his backpack, opened it, pulled out a foil blanket and wrapped it around Ash. He pushed something into Ash's hands. "Here. Eat. Then we'll go."

Everything in fragments. Dad hugging him, stubble rough against his skin. The tension in Dad's body, in his voice. Then hot sweet tea from a thermos. Chunks of flapjack. Slowly, very slowly, a little of Ash's strength started to come back.

"Better?" Dad asked.

"Yes," said Ash. "A little. Thanks."

"Good. Now, the rescue team headed off toward Black Crag. They won't be back yet, and getting around the wildfire will slow them down."

Ash nodded. "We have to hurry, get Mark and get away quickly in case the wind changes direction again and the wildfire cuts off our way back down."

"I know," said Dad. "I'll try calling mountain rescue, see if they'll send another team out to us."

He tried his phone, frowned. "No signal."

"There's never a signal out here," said Ash. "It's a black spot."

"No phones, then," said Dad. "Right. It'll take us about an hour to get back down to the road. Maybe longer in these conditions and with you so exhausted. Could be two hours minimum, and the same again to get the team back up here, assuming the wind keeps the fire to the west of us. Mark might not last that long."

Dad was talking too fast, panicking again.

"Dad," said Ash, "slow down. Please."

"You said that Mark was conscious when you left him. Do you think he can hang on down there for a few more hours while we get help?"

"I don't know," said Ash. "He was hurt pretty badly."

"Okay," said Dad. "I brought my climbing gear, in case you'd fallen somewhere. We'll have to get him off the mountain ourselves."

Of course. Dad, the army officer, the mountain man, the climber. He'd come to rescue Ash in the mountains; he'd come prepared. Still the same old Dad deep inside, in

216

spite of everything. For a moment, Ash felt safe, as if Dad could do anything, save him, save Mark, save all of them.

Except he also knew Dad could lose it at any moment, freak out, run away, hide.

For now, at least, he didn't. For now, they were a team. Together they could do this.

"I need you to show me exactly where Mark is," Dad said. "Think you can manage that?"

Ash nodded. "Yeah."

Dad helped him to his feet. He stood swaying, gathering himself. Then he looked around.

The full moon burned through a gap in the clouds.

They set off toward the edge of Stag's Leap. The wind in their faces. Ash half-delirious with exhaustion, his body bruised and battered and aching all over. But none of that mattered. He had to keep going.

"That's where Mark is," said Ash as they got closer. "Right below there. The ledge is about fifteen feet down."

Dad went out onto the Leap. Then he lay down and looked over the edge. "Okay," he said. "A straight drop, about fifteen feet, like you said. The ledge looks pretty wide where Mark's lying."

Then Dad was on his feet again. The wind gusted and Ash swayed again, braced himself.

Dad stood in front of him. "Are you all right?"

"Yeah. Just really tired."

"Hang in there a little while longer, son. We'll all be home soon."

Ash felt sick with nerves. Anything could go wrong. Mark

might already be dead. Dad might fall. But he couldn't let Dad know how worried he was so he kept quiet and nodded.

"How on earth did you climb up that rock face without a rope?" said Dad. "It looks sheer from the top."

Ash shrugged and looked down. "There's handholds, toeholds. I just sort of did it, the way you taught me."

"Amazing," said Dad. "Really. I'm proud of you."

"Thanks."

"Listen, I could see Mark when I looked over the edge but he wasn't moving. That probably means he's either too weak or he's lost consciousness since you left him. So I'm going to go down there and between us we're going to get him up. I'll take the spare harness for Mark and rig the ropes so you can help me by taking some of Mark's weight as I bring him back up. Okay? Do you think you can handle it?"

"Yeah, I can handle it."

"All right then."

"Dad," said Ash, "what if it's like the other day when we went fishing and you thought there were snipers? What if you get flashbacks again?"

"I'm all right," said Dad. "I can do it."

"Okay," said Ash. "What can I do?"

"Stay a few feet back from the edge. I'll set up the ropes and when I give the signal, start pulling. Slow and steady, don't yank the rope."

Ash nodded. Exhaustion washed through him again. His vision blurred and his eyelids slid shut. He forced them open, focused his eyes. Dad was already pulling his climbing gear from his backpack. Ash watched as he fixed the anchors, clipped himself into his harness, rolled out ropes.

Dad handed him a pair of gloves and Ash took hold of the rope.

"Okay," said Dad. "My rope is anchored so you don't need to worry about that. The rope you're holding will take some of Mark's weight so you'll need to be ready. I'll give you a shout but pay attention to the rope in case you can't hear me. When you feel it go taut, start pulling steadily like I told you. Ready?"

"Ready."

Then Ash watched as Dad disappeared over the edge of the Leap.

IT SEEMED TO ASH THAT he kept falling asleep over and over, on his feet, and that each time he woke everything was almost exactly the same. Minutes passed, hours, months, years, centuries, and nothing changed. The rope in his gloved hands, the rain still falling, the wind in his face. There was no weight on the rope yet, but that would come soon and when it did, he'd be ready.

The wildfire was still moving westward, away from them. Dad was still over the edge, swinging down the rock face into a storm.

Ash was too tired to make sense of it anymore. All he wanted was to sleep but he couldn't, not yet. Not until all this was over.

Mark had to be all right. He just *had* to be.

Just then Ash heard Dad shout.

Ash pulled slow and steady, like Dad said.

He tilted his weight back, bracing against the rope, pulled hand over hand, grunting with the effort.

Everything hurt. His muscles taut with pain, his shoulder throbbing, his legs and arms trembling.

It seemed like an age passed. Then finally Ash saw Dad

clamber up over the edge, turn and reach down, then haul Mark up and over. At last, they sprawled onto the flat ground.

Ash let go of the rope and went to them.

Mark was conscious but loose as a rag doll, his face gaunt. As carefully as they could, Ash and his dad dragged Mark away from the edge.

Dad unstrapped himself from the harness, pulled up the dangling ropes. Then, as if a switch had been flipped, he started fidgeting, pacing, all edgy now. "He's in bad shape," he said of Mark. "His shoulder's smashed up and there could be any number of other problems. Head injury, spinal injury, internal bleeding, hypothermia. Anything." Dad was talking too fast. "We should have a stretcher, a helicopter. We need a damn helicopter. Where the hell is the helicopter?"

"They don't know where we are, remember," said Ash. "They don't know where we are and we have no way of telling them so we have to get him down the mountain ourselves. Dad, we can do this. Okay? Just take a deep breath. All right?"

Dad stopped pacing. He drew a deep shaky breath. "Okay," he said. "I'm okay. You're right."

But then Dad just stood there, staring down at Mark, doing nothing.

"Dad," said Ash. "Give me the rope."

"The rope." His voice blank, as if his mind was elsewhere and he was repeating the words without understanding them.

"We've got to make a stretcher for Mark," said Ash. "So we can carry him down the mountain. Remember? We're going to make it the way you showed me when I was a kid, out of rope and a bivvy bag. So I need the rope."

Dad still looked out of it but he nodded slowly and handed Ash the rope.

Ash looped the rope on the ground to make a stretcher, the way he remembered Dad teaching him on one of those weekends he had taken Ash out into the mountains to camp and climb and learn survival skills. Then he looked in Dad's backpack for a bivvy bag and anything else they could use to wrap up Mark.

He found the bag and a foil blanket and laid them out over the stretcher. "Okay," he said. "It's ready."

Carefully Ash and Dad lifted Mark onto it. Mark sobbed with pain but didn't scream, didn't try to make them stop.

They wrapped the foil and the bivvy bag over him, then Dad laced the ropes around so Mark was cocooned.

"How are you doing, Mark?" said Ash.

"I'm okay," he said. But his voice was barely a whisper.

"Good. Now hang on," said Ash. "We're going to get you down."

Then Dad took hold of the front end of the stretcher and Ash took the other end, slipping his hands under and through the looped rope, and together they set off down the eastern slope of the Leap.

34

ASH WALKED. HE WALKED IN the footsteps of long-dead shepherds and hunters, warriors and poets, peddlers and wanderers, lovers, wisewomen, outlaws, rebels. He'd never felt them around him before, but even time seemed different now, the land giving up its ghosts and its memories. It was as if the centuries that separated him from them were vapor-thin.

The banshee wind screamed in his ears.

He dreamed the names of peak and dip and rise and boulder, and they sang through him. The story of the land, written in rock and blood and wraith. Through Silent Hollow, where the path curved into the long shallow trough of Houndgrave, and on past Burntwood, where no trees grew; past the Keening Stone, a big teardrop of rock with a smooth round hole that the wind wailed through.

Ash raised his face into the storm.

He glanced at Dad up ahead. At Mark, swaddled in the bivvy bag, his face ghostly pale.

He looked to his right and saw Bone Jack suddenly there.

"Are you really here?" he said.

"Aye."

"Why have you come?"

"To see things through as they're meant to be."

"Can they see you too? Dad and Mark?"

But Bone Jack didn't answer.

Ash kept walking. Tired beyond tired. He scarcely felt it anymore. He zoned in and out. He was borne along by storm and gravity, by willpower, by some ancient instinct of his body.

In the distance, the wildfire was a line of dirty orange that surged and shimmered.

His mind drifted into dreams. He was running barefoot through steady rain, along mountain paths claggy with mud. In this dream, someone ran beside him, but when he turned to see who it was, no one was there.

Ash stumbled, caught himself. Looked up. The bitter smell of smoke filled his nose and mouth.

"We've been walking for hours," he said to Bone Jack. "We've hardly gotten anywhere."

"It's only been a few minutes," said Bone Jack. "Keep on, lad."

Ash walked. But the world seemed faraway and nothing to do with him, like he didn't belong to it anymore.

Still. He walked on.

He watched the wildfire. It seemed brighter, closer. Then Ash realized—the wind had changed direction again, driving the fire back toward them. It roared like the ocean, eating up the land, smoke rolling over it like low cloud. Rain couldn't stop it. Men couldn't stop it. The land would burn until there was nothing left to burn.

"Are we going to die?" said Ash. His teeth chattered, though he no longer felt cold. "Are we going to get down off this mountain?"

Bone Jack didn't answer. Ash looked over at him but he was gone, vanished into the night. If he'd ever really been there at all.

Ash and Dad kept walking, slow and steady, bearing Mark's weight down the mountainside. Ash's thoughts drifted back over everything that had happened: Mark, the ghostly hound boys, the mysterious stag boy who'd shown him how to climb back up the rock face, Bone Jack and the wolf. And Dad, coming up to the Leap to find him. Somehow Dad had known where he'd be. But how?

"Dad," he said.

"Yeah?"

"Why didn't you go with the rescue team? Why did you come up to the Leap instead?"

Dad turned to look at Ash as best he could. "Just a wild guess."

"It was a good guess."

"I went to Tom's grave before the start of the race," said Dad. "Like you did."

"Mom told you."

"Yeah. I saw the photograph: me and Tom and you and Mark and Callie when you were little. Up on the Leap. When you didn't come down from the mountains with the others, I knew something was wrong and I couldn't get that photo out of my mind. It seemed like a message, a message from Tom. That picture of us all up on Stag's Leap, then that day when I was the stag boy and Tom saved my life. On the Leap, again. And, well, now here we are."

"Here we are."

Ash was about to say more, but the sight of a distant thorn tree bright with flames stopped him.

"Dad," said Ash. "The wildfire."

"I know," said Dad, his voice rough-edged and tense again.

"We have to go. Keep moving," said Ash. His head bent into the weltering storm, trudging on, steady, relentless. "We're all right. We'll make it."

And there was only Ash, Dad, and Mark, and a choking blizzard of rain and ember and ash and the wildfire beyond them like the end of the world.

Until finally they were past it, the wildfire hungering southward while they skirted its charred and smoldering flank.

35

THERE WERE LIGHTS IN THE valley. Flashlights, and the headlights of cars. Men in red mountain jackets and hard hats ran up to meet them. They brought a proper stretcher, unswaddled Mark, fitted braces to his back and neck and took him away. Blue lights flashing, a siren wailing. Ash watched through his eyelashes.

Then Mom was there too, hugging him so hard he could hardly breathe.

The paramedics put him in the back of a Land Rover ambulance. Voices. Warmth. Mom and Dad standing at the door, watching him. The growl of an engine. Someone checking him over. A blood-pressure cuff tightening around his arm. The door closed. The ambulance bumped down the road.

Ash drifted in and out of sleep.

A white glare. White walls. Bright steel. A metallic rattling noise.

Faces he didn't recognize. A nurse looking down at him. More voices.

A bed in a big half-dark room. He curled up on his side, in the deep warmth of blankets, and slept again.

Later, he woke to daylight.

"Hi, sweetie," said Mom. "Are you all right?"

"Mom," he said. His mind still fogged with sleep. "What time is it?"

She smiled. "About ten o'clock, I think."

"In the morning?"

"Yes, darling, in the morning."

The smell of antiseptic. On the wall behind her there was a tall white cabinet, a sink, double doors. Ash looked around. In a bed opposite, an older-looking man slept propped against several pillows.

At the other end of the room, two more beds. Both empty.

"I'm in a hospital," he said. His voice was a rough whisper, his throat dry and sore.

"Do you remember what happened?"

"Yeah," he said. "Sort of. Parts of it anyway."

"You were suffering from exhaustion and mild hypothermia so they kept you overnight for observation. They think you might have a slight concussion too, and you'll have a sore throat and a cough for a few days from the smoke inhalation. You've got some nasty cuts and deep bruising as well, especially around your shoulder, but nothing is broken. You are very lucky. You could have been killed."

"I wasn't, though." He could hardly believe it. "I'm here, I'm alive. But it wasn't luck. It was . . ." Mark. The stag boy. Bone Jack. Only he couldn't tell Mom about that stuff. "Dad," he said. "Dad found us. He got Mark up from the ledge but then he started losing it. But it was okay. I kept him calm and kept us going all the way down from the mountain."

"I know. I was there when you came down." She smiled. "You did great. And the doctor gave you the all-clear to come home today, so long as you promise to rest."

"I will. Where's Dad?"

"He was here most of the night. He was exhausted himself but he sat with you for hours. We both did."

"Is he okay?" said Ash.

"All the strain was tough on him. The hospital, you know. Mr. Sloper gave him a ride home a little while ago."

"But Dad came to the Stag Chase in the end, didn't he? I mean, before he knew something had gone wrong in the mountains? He came to see me run?"

"Yes, he did."

"He wasn't afraid."

"He was," she said. "But he came anyway. He wanted to stop off at Tom Cullen's grave, like you did, and you'd already set off by the time we arrived. We waited, so we'd be there when you finished. Then later, when we realized you were missing and there was a storm, he went into action. We drove straight back home so he could pick up his mountain gear, then he went out looking for you."

Ash paused. "So maybe, eventually, he really will be all right?"

"He'll have his good days and bad," she said. "It's going

to take time. Maybe a very long time. He's going to talk to a counselor later this week. It's a start. Hopefully, things will get better, bit by bit."

Ash nodded. "Where's Mark? Is he . . . ?"

Alive, alive. He couldn't say the word.

"Mark will be fine," Mom said. "He's got a concussion too, and a few broken bones. He'll have to stay in the hospital for a while longer, a couple weeks maybe, but he should make a full recovery. Callie's with him now." She paused. "Oh and I spoke to their grandpa earlier."

"Spoke to him? How?"

She laughed. "The same way I'm speaking to you. He's sick. He's not dead. Anyway, Callie might come and stay with us for a while, just until things are sorted out. Would that be all right with you?"

"Yeah," he said. "Of course. What about Mark? What will happen to him?"

"Well, if his grandpa continues to improve, he could be discharged in a few days, so hopefully he'll be back home by the time Mark is released. Mark will probably want to move back in with him, for a while anyway."

"We're going to be all right, Mom. Aren't we?"

"Yes, we're going to be all right."

Finally Ash drew a deep breath and let it out slowly.

36

AFTER HE HAD DRESSED, ASH and his mom walked slowly along the hospital corridor. Past doors that led to other rooms and wards. They walked through a throng of anxious visitors and busy nurses, and patients swinging along on crutches. They went through a set of double doors into a corridor with a mural of a deep dark forest painted along the length of both walls. They passed a wolf and a crow and a moonlit waterfall and an owl with great golden eyes. They went through a blue door into a room with only one bed in it.

Callie was sitting at the bedside. Mark was lying on his back. One leg splinted and elevated. His shoulder was in a cast, his head bandaged, his eyes closed. He looked smaller, frail. A tube from a drip bag fed into a vein on his forearm. Wires. A monitor of some sort.

Ash stood in the doorway, stared at him. Best friend. Enemy. The boy who'd tried to kill him. The boy who'd tried to save him. The boy he'd helped to save.

"Has he woken up at all yet?" said Mom.

Callie was watching Mark. She didn't look around. "Yes, about an hour ago," she said. "The nurses came and checked him. He's just sleeping now."

Mom touched Ash's arm. "I'm going to make a few phone calls, give you some time to yourselves. I'll be back in a bit."

"Okay."

Ash stepped forward into the room. "How's he doing?"

Callie didn't answer. Her gaze never left Mark.

"The doctors told my mom he'll be all right," Ash said. "Mostly just a few broken bones."

Callie looked at him then. Her fragile bony face. Eyes huge with tiredness and worry. "He's not all right," she said. "He's alive but he's not all right."

"My mom said he'll probably be home in a couple weeks."

"We don't have a home."

Ash didn't answer. Didn't know what to say. It hit him then that Mark was all Callie had left in the world. Her parents were dead. Grandpa Cullen was still in the hospital. There was no one else. Just her and Mark. And Mark's grief—the madness of it—had eclipsed Callie's, left her desolate on the sideline.

There was another chair by the window. Ash sat in it, glanced outside across the tops of tall pine trees where crows flapped and tumbled in the wind.

"You look tired," he said.

"I've been up all night."

"Mom says you can stay with us," he said. "You know, until things are sorted out."

"Until what things are sorted out? Who's going to sort them?"

Ash shrugged. "I don't know. Your grandpa, I guess. Have you seen him yet?"

"Yes. They brought him down to visit Mark last night. He's doing a lot better."

Then, silence. Callie's gaze steady on Mark. At last she said, "What happened up there?"

"He caught up with me on Stag's Leap. We fought and we got too close to the edge."

"Did he try to kill you?"

Ash was quiet for a long moment. "It started out like that," he said. "Yeah. He kept slamming into me, trying to push me off the Leap. He nearly succeeded. Then he stopped, right at the edge. When it came down to it, he couldn't go through with it."

"What happened, then? How did you fall?"

"We were too close to the edge and the wind was so strong up there with the rain hammering down and the ghost boys mobbing us. I lost my footing. Mark tried to save me. He grabbed my wrist and tried to pull me back, away from the edge, but I was already falling so he fell with me."

"I'm sorry," she said. "All that stuff he was talking about, blood for blood and life for life. It scared me but I never thought he'd actually go through with it."

"He didn't go through with it," said Ash. "In the end, he didn't. You were right. He's not a killer. He's just messed up right now. I don't think most of it was his doing anyway."

"What do you mean?"

"Those ghost hound boys. Bone Jack told me that they

hunt the stag boy every year, only most years they're weak, not much more than mountain mist. This year they were strong, though. The foot-and-mouth, the slaughter, the drought, your dad, all that sort of amplified them, made them stronger. They fed off all that darkness. It made them strong enough to kill and they almost did."

Callie looked at him with something like gratitude. "You saved Mark's life," she said. "You could have waited on the ledge until the search party found you and Mark probably would have died. But instead you risked your life and you climbed up, went to get help."

Ash looked away, embarrassed. "Yeah, well. I couldn't let him die out there."

"Do you think it's over now?" said Callie.

Ash gazed out the window again. The gray sky, the pine trees jagged and black against it.

"I hope so. The hounds are back where they belong. The rain came. The drought's over and the wildfire's probably burned out by now. The land will heal in time."

In the bed, Mark moved, cried out in his sleep.

They stared at him.

His eyelids flickered. His eyes half opened. He looked at them for a long time. Then he whispered something, his voice so weak that they couldn't make out the words.

Callie took Mark's hand in hers. They sat with him, said nothing. His eyes closed.

He was asleep again by the time Mom came back.

"How's he doing?" she asked.

"He woke up," said Ash. "Only for a second, though."

"Why don't we leave him to rest now," said Mom. "Let's get you home. You too, Callie. We'll come back tomorrow, during visiting hours."

"I want to stay with Mark," said Callie.

But Mom shook her head. "You need something to eat and a hot bath and a good night's sleep. Mark's in good hands. The best thing you can do for him right now is take care of yourself."

Ash expected Callie to argue, for all that stubborn fire inside her to blaze up. But instead she nodded, stood up. In her torn and muddy dress, her dark hair still wind-knotted, she looked like a lost child.

"Home it is, then," said Mom.

37

THE CURTAINS AND WINDOW WERE open, the clouds had lifted, and sunlight was pouring into the spare room where Dad had been sleeping. All the junk was gone, moved to the garage. A red rug lay on the floor, the bed had been made up with clean sheets, a duvet.

Callie stood in the doorway, watching Dad angle a little bedside table into place.

Dad looked rough but he smiled at her. "Will this be okay for you?" he said.

Callie nodded solemnly. "Thanks."

"Tomorrow we'll visit your grandpa in the hospital and arrange to pick up your things from his house," said Dad. "You'll feel more at home when you've got your own things around you."

Outside the window, a crow perched on a branch of the old apple tree and preened its feathers in the soft light.

Dad and Callie watched the bird, and Ash watched Dad and Callie and thought how they were both broken but both still standing, sometimes faltering, falling, yet getting up again, continuing on. And Ash was part of that too. This time he hadn't run away from problems, the way he'd done with Mark when his father had died. He'd wanted to but he hadn't. Ash had stood by them, done what he had to do, helped to bring them all home. And he'd do it again if he had to, again and again because although it wasn't easy, it was simple. You stood by the people you loved and you did whatever you had to do to help them.

Ash. left them there, went outside and sat on the bench at the front of the house. Dark clouds were gathering over Tolley Carn, another storm on its way. Beyond it, he saw blackened slopes where the wildfire had burned itself out. Here and there, faint scarves of smoke trailed where the land still smoldered.

A crow winged past.

Where was Bone Jack now? Ash wondered. Was he still out there, wandering in the mountains? Where were the ghostly stag boy, the hounds, the wolf?

Then a voice in Ash's head:

Back where they belong, it said. *Back where it's quiet, where they can rest.*

The next day, Ash stood with Dad in the hospital corridor, watching Mark through the glass pane in the door. Mark looked smashed and hollowed out, his summer burn faded under the stark hospital lights. He no longer looked like the savage, half-crazed creature he'd become in the mountains but to Ash he still seemed more like a stranger than the Mark who'd once been his best friend.

But he knew the old Mark was still there, inside that broken body, and there was something still unfinished between them. Something that Ash needed to know.

"It's okay to go in," said Dad. "But don't be too long. He's still not himself."

Ash nodded, drew a deep breath and went into Mark's room.

Mark opened his eyes. They two boys looked at each other. After a moment Ash asked the question that had been on his mind ever since he and Dad had rescued Mark from the ledge. "Why didn't you kill me?"

The wind keened at the window. Gray sky, a slash of rain glittering on the glass.

Summer was over.

Mark still strapped into casts, eyes closed now, tears silvering his cheeks.

"Why didn't you kill me?" Ash repeated. "Why did you change your mind?"

Nothing.

"I need to know."

"I almost did kill you," said Mark.

"I know. Then you stopped and tried to save me. Why?"

A long silence, then Mark started to talk. "You remember when my mom died? It was a long time ago. But I remember all of it. It was like part of my dad died too, when Mom did. Like we lost them both. He hardly ever smiled after that. He just worked. All the time. And then last year there was foot-and-mouth and I was out there for hours with him, day after day, bringing our sheep down from the mountains, watching the government workers kill them, watching them burn. He couldn't take it."

Ash shifted uncomfortably in his seat, the memories flooding back. All that loss, all that pain and horror. "Callie told me you're the one who found him."

"Yeah, well, she doesn't know everything. There was more to it than that."

"What do you mean?"

"My dad was still alive when I went into the barn. He was up there in the hayloft, where you and I used to mess around. He'd already tied the rope to a rafter. He had the noose around his neck. And I went in and I guess I yelled or something because he looked straight at me. Straight at me, Ash. And then he jumped anyway."

Ash couldn't breathe, couldn't speak. In his mind's eye he saw it all. The barn at night, Mark going in, looking up. And Tom Cullen, his expression cold and faraway, already out of reach. Then falling through the darkness.

The crack of his neck breaking.

"I'm so sorry," said Ash softly.

And there was no need for Mark to tell him any more. Ash knew it all now. Why Mark couldn't get his dad's death out of his head. How he'd tried to erase it, make his dad's death unhappen. Why he felt like he had to find a way to save him. How everything had gotten jumbled up in the madness of Mark's grief: the folktales his dad and grandpa used to tell, the Stag Chase, the ghostly hound boys drawn to his pain, no more than breaths of mist at first but growing stronger all the time.

But in the end, Mark had chosen life and the living over the dead.

"Thanks for telling me," said Ash.

Mark nodded. "So what happens now?" he said.

"We live our lives, I guess," said Ash. "One foot forward, then the other."

Mark gave a weak smile. "So cheesy."

"I know," said Ash. "It works, though. You just keep going until you get to where you need to be. That's all we can do. That's how we got you down off the mountain."

"I don't remember any of that," said Mark. "But I remember trying to push you off the Leap. There was this look in your eyes, like you still couldn't believe I'd really go through with it, even though you were inches from the edge. Like you still trusted me somehow. Then when you told me about how my dad saved your dad suddenly it was like I was standing outside myself, watching this crazy person trying to kill you, and I knew I couldn't do it. I knew my dad wouldn't want that. I remember the hounds pushing us over the edge, but after that I don't remember anything until I woke up here. How did you climb up?"

"It was the stag boy," said Ash. "The ghost stag boy. They must have hunted him up there, centuries ago, and he fell off the Leap too and landed on the same ledge we did, and he climbed up. He showed me the way. He had survived, so I knew we could too."

Tears glittered on Mark's cheeks again. "I'm sorry," he said. "I'm so sorry."

"It's okay," said Ash. "We're okay. We both made it back."

A knock at the door. Dad came in. "You ready?"

"Yeah," said Ash. He stood up, looked at Mark. "I'll come back tomorrow, if you want."

Mark smiled. "Yeah. That would be good."

ONE FOOT IN FRONT OF the other.

Days turned into months. Early November. The chill of fall was now in the air.

The leaves on the beech trees shone like copper shields. The nights were drawing in and the mountains were ghostly with low cloud. Soon there would be snow on the high peaks, ice cracking underfoot.

One day Ash found Callie in the garden, crouched. In her cupped hands was a tiny brown bird, loose with death. Its eye was still gleaming, a bead of bright blood on its beak.

"It flew into the window," she said, and sobs shook through her.

Ash touched her shoulder. When she turned away, he stood there with her for a moment. Then he went back inside the house.

There were no races he could run for her, no trophies he could lay at her feet.

There was only damage that would take a long time to heal.

From his bed, Ash watched the trees move in the wind.

He thought about Callie, and the bird. He thought about Mark, the stag boy, Bone Jack.

It still wasn't over. Not yet.

Later that morning Ash walked up the road, past winter-black trees and silent fields, along the old drovers' paths through the mountains to Corbie Tor.

All the way there, he thought about turning back. The Stag Chase was over and done with and he should move on with his life. But part of him didn't want to leave it in the past, at least not entirely. He had touched the edges of mystery and it had swirled about him for a while, changing everything. He didn't want to forget.

In the valley below, the sluggish stream of summer had become a little rushing river, sparkling in the late-morning sunlight. The autumn winds had stripped most of the leaves from the thorn trees. Heavy clusters of hawthorns the color of dried blood hung among their dark boughs.

Ash went down, jumped rock to rock across the river, pushed his way through the thorn trees to the old stone hut with its grimy windows and the bone strings rattling in the doorway.

A crow flapped down and settled on a branch. Then another, and another. They shook out their feathers and filled the air with their rough cries. He waited, half expecting Bone Jack to appear through the trees, but Bone Jack didn't come.

Ash stood outside the doorway in a drift of dead leaves. He hesitated. Then he stepped inside.

No one was there. Everything was as he remembered it: the fox skull on the shelf, the old army knife, the flint arrowheads. The book.

The book he'd taken the last time he came, the old copy of *The Battle of the Trees* that the wind had ripped apart in his hands. Only now it was intact once more, and back where he'd found it. It lay open to the page Ash remembered well.

> I have been in a multitude of shapes,
> Before I assumed a consistent form.

Ash closed the book and went outside.

The autumn sun sat low over the mountains.

The mew of a buzzard.

A cold wind blowing.

Ash ran. Ran past Corbie Tor and along the high paths and soon a shadow ran with him, a shadow that became a clay-daubed boy with a great wolf racing at his side. And Ash and the stag boy ran and laughed for the joy of it, for the wildness of it, for the fierce beauty of the wolf and for the story of the land that had not yet ended, that would never end.

ACKNOWLEDGMENTS AND AUTHOR'S NOTE

Special thanks go to my agent Joanna Swainson, my editors Eloise Wilson, Liza Kaplan, Charlie Sheppard, and Ruth Knowles.

The lines from *Cad Goddeu* (*The Battle of the Trees*) used in *Bone Jack* are taken from William F. Skene's translation in *The Four Ancient Books of Wales* (1868).